FLYING DUTCHMAN
SUNSET STATION
BOOK 3

GENE DOUCETTE

Flying Dutchman

Copyright © 2026 Gene Doucette
All rights reserved

Cover by Kim Killion
***This book may not be reproduced by any means including but not
limited to photocopy, digital, auditory, and/or in print.***

SANDEE

"KRIS? Kris, now's not the time," Sandee said. "You've gotta get out of there."

Kris Standard, currently aboard an alien spaceship behind a sealed airlock door and running out of oxygen way faster than she should be, had just decided to take a nap. And there wasn't anything Sandee could do about it, other than shout about how much of a bad idea that was.

Meanwhile, everyone else was spinning out of control in their own special way. Davina, at the stick in the shuttle, was trying to get it into position for Josip—in the shuttle's airlock—to spacewalk his way over to Alan, who was free-floating and unconscious after getting knocked around in the violent closure of the alien ship's airlock door.

According to the string of curse words Josip kept rattling off on his dedicated line, Davina wasn't piloting the shuttle particularly well at the moment. This made sense, as Dav was busy asking Sandee for an update on Kris every few seconds.

Paul, meanwhile, was in the hub, prepping to receive Alan. He kept asking Sandee if she knew any more than he did about

Alan's condition, like that was something she'd know from just looking at Alan on the viewscreen.

Then there was Monterrey, which kept trying to break in for an update on *everyone*, but probably especially Kris, because Kris's suit alarms were lighting up her whole biofeed screen.

Sandee couldn't do much of anything about all of *that* either.

"Kris, can you hear me?" Sandee asked. "Kris, I really need you to talk to me."

"*How can I help?*" Susie the Support Bot asked.

"I don't think you can, Susie, but thanks," Sandee said.

"*Of course!*"

"Kris?" Sandee asked again. "Need you to wake up, girl."

There was no answer.

Focus on what you can control, Sandee thought, taking a deep breath. If Kris was taking a nap, she was taking a nap, and that was all there was to it. Sandee pushed a repetitive *ping* to Kris's suit, took a couple more calming breaths, and concentrated on untangling everything else that was going wrong.

She opened a line to Paul.

"Jo's two meters from Alan now, Paul," she said. "Everything looks smooth. I'll make sure you're patched into the airlock over there as soon as they're back inside."

"But how does he look?" Paul asked.

"Like an unconscious dude in a spacesuit. Not much more to tell."

"Roger that, how's Kris?"

Sandee disconnected rather than answer.

Outside, the shuttle had caught up with Alan. Sandee switched to the shuttle's external feed and watched as Josip pushed out of the airlock and—after some tense seconds—caught Alan, while managing not to get bisected by the spinning tether cord still attached to Alan's belt.

"I have him," Josip said, hitting reverse on the winch in the airlock to reel the two of them in. This would take a while, because momentum was not their friend.

Knowing Davina would be free, Sandee toggled to Dav's private line.

"Hey, Dav," she said. "So, about Kris."

"Is she okay??"

"I don't know how to answer that," Sandee admitted. "Like, yeah, her vitals show she's still alive, but she's not awake and what I'm seeing is she only has about ninety minutes of air."

"She should have much more than that," Davina said.

"I know. But look, I'm thinking mine's not the best voice to wake her up. Maybe if she hears *you*..."

"Patch me through."

"Can you handle the shuttle *and* talk to her? I'm saying..."

"Jo can take over as soon as Alan is secure. Patch me through."

"All right, here you go. Hey, ah, I'm gonna record you two, okay? Just, well if it's the last..."

"It's fine," Davina said. "Set it up."

It took a minute to arrange the communication lines appropriately—Dav's private channel had to go back to the hub, then out to Kris's private channel, without interfering with the channel Sandee had going with Kris already, and without going to a line Monterrey could listen in on. They didn't need potentially the whole world eavesdropping on their last conversation together, and Sandee no longer trusted anyone from mission control to behave with anything like tact or decency.

Speaking of, once she'd set that up, it was time to update Monterrey. Sandee unmuted the direct from the surface.

"Hey, Mo, it's Sandee," she said. "How you guys doing down there?"

"We need updates," Morris said. "Make the data we're looking at down here make sense."

"Sure thing, but I think you better switch us to a private line first. Not sure the whole control room wants to hear what I have to say."

"Go on."

"You don't want me to elaborate, Mo. Not on an open call. Take me to your office or this conversation's gonna get messy."

There was a long pause, and then, "Roger that," he said. "Give me two minutes."

MORRIS

AS A CHILD OF THE INTERNET, Morris Esteban had developed a set of rules he would later call the Bullshit Toolbox, as a means to navigate the various "truths" that routinely popped up online. *Most* of the rules were pretty obvious, and still mostly worked, such as:

- don't believe outrageous claims without verifying first;
- the photo you're looking at has probably been manipulated, and;
- she's just a bot.

Some were too specific, and/or had become dated, like:

- don't let a stranger drive you somewhere, or;
- stop answering texts from Janey Kittle.

One particular Bullshit Toolbox rule had been on his mind a lot of late. It was a rule that should absolutely still stand up, and yet he was increasingly concerned that it would not.

The rule was, that there's an inverse proportion to the number of people who would have to be involved in a conspiracy for it to succeed and the likelihood of it being real. Basically, if a conspiracy can work with only five people knowing, then sure, it's possible. But, it's not much of a conspiracy either. For it to be a *proper* conspiracy, it'd need the tacit involvement of dozens-to-hundreds of people, and that was way too many.

But that was before Mo ended up on the inside of one such conspiracy, wherein a division of the Ellis PR team *invented* an alien encounter scenario that absolutely did not happen. The fact that the lie seemed to have stuck had Mo wondering if he'd been naïve—that his rule had *never* been true—or if it was only true in a time before a single conglomerate had control over more than half the world's media consumables.

Unless he was writing off the rule prematurely. Because the reason Morris considered a true conspiracy unlikely was that the more people who knew the lie, the more opportunities there were for that lie to be exposed, and the first opportunity for that exposure surfaced only a week later.

WHEN MAX TOLD Morris about the plan, Mo nearly quit on the spot.

"In two days, we're going to announce that Sunset Station has made positive contact with the aliens," Max told him. "And, importantly, that they will only speak to us."

This was a conversation between Mo and Max only. The other members of the team (a total of thirty-seven people in mission control *had* to be in on it, if it was to work) would be told next, but Max had to break it to Morris first, because he'd need Morris's help to get everyone else on board.

"Why would we do that?" Mo asked. "Unless I missed something, it's not true."

"I'm buying us alone time with the EAS. That's all."

"By lying."

"It's a premature truth," Max said. "I have all the confidence in the world that the Sunset Station team, supported by Monterrey mission control, can turn first contact into a reality."

"*Nobody* is going to believe it," Morris said, which—he would admit to himself later—was an awfully weak rejoinder. He was too busy in the moment being stunned that he was hearing this at all.

"Enough will to believe it to buy us the time we need," Max said. "Once we've made contact, we'll retrofit what the aliens actually have to say with whatever anodyne *kumbaya* the writers *said* they said. It'll work out, I promise."

"I'm sorry, I think I'm losing my mind right now. I'm a *scientist*, Max. So are all the people in that control room. So is everyone in orbit. Verifiably true things are very much life-and-death matters for us, *especially* with a team in space. If you think anyone here is willing and *able* to stand up in front of the world and say..."

"No, no, no," Max interrupted. "You don't have to do anything like that. The EAS PR team is handling everything. All I need is for nobody *here* to counterprogram the message. We'll be passing out updated NDAs today, with a new bonus structure we figure will help."

"You can't... Max. You can't *force* something to be true that isn't."

Max laughed. "Again: it's not untrue; it's *prematurely* true. And of course I can."

Morris agreed to go along with the plan, but he also drafted a letter of resignation and put it in a desktop folder called "things I hope to never have a use for." Like everything else in that folder—such as a medical DNR and a list of his logon passwords for his next-of-kin—he hoped to never have to use it.

WHO CALLED bullshit was a real surprise. Mo expected someone in the media to get the story, and was deeply concerned about being the one responsible for confirming the facts of the lie. He'd gotten in the habit of letting every call go to his voicemail—even ones ostensibly from people he knew—and hadn't left the Monterrey campus for any reason, (although he would have needed dispensation to do so) to reduce the odds of a chance encounter with someone who Just Had A Couple of Questions. *On* campus, he avoided people who worked for Ellis Aero but who weren't in on the conspiracy.

He thought he was covered.

Then Sandee—one of the six most information-starved people on or off the planet—pulled him into a private conversation, told him she knew what they'd been doing, and dared Morris to tell her something different.

Which he did not do, because there was obviously no point, as she was also one of the six people on or off the planet who knew without a doubt that Sunset Station wasn't talking to any aliens.

And that wasn't even the worst part of what Sandee had to tell him.

"What do you *mean*, they're all dead?" he asked Sandee. It was at her suggestion that he'd switched their conversation to a private line in his office. This was a consideration she absolutely did not have to give, but more than anyone else in space at the moment, Sandee was a savvy political animal. Rather than call out the lie to a roomful of people—and risk being heard by someone *unaware* that the Sunset Station team had not, in fact, been trading recipes with the aliens for the past week—she preemptively compartmentalized. Good instinct, and also? Maybe Max's lie was going to survive a little longer.

"I mean," she said, "that according to Kris there are six aliens on that ship, and all of 'em are dead, so you better tell Max to retrofit that bogus friendly neighborhood space alien shit he's pitching."

"Uh, okay. Okay. How *is* Kris? The readings we're getting on her aren't great."

"I know," Sandee said. "I'm looking at the same thing. I think she passed out from gravity sickness. She's also about to run out of oxygen, and we have no way to get in there to help, in anything less than the time it'll take for her to run out. She's pretty much on her own for now. Maybe I should've led with that."

"I'm going to hand you back to the control room," Morris said. "Give them a full breakdown, please. Everything except the part about the dead aliens. Maybe together we can figure out how to get to Kris before it's too late."

"Roger that. Hey, she's pulled off the impossible once before, yeah?"

"Sure. Let's just hope she didn't use up all her luck."

Morris passed Sandee off to Adrian, in the control room. Then he opened his bottom drawer, took out a gifted bottle of scotch (he hated scotch) and took a swig. Then he pulled the resignation letter out of its folder, dropped it into an email, and hit send. Then he picked up the phone and called Max.

MAX

MAX WAS BUSY, staring angrily at a printed report that wasn't telling him what he wanted it to tell him.

The existence of the report in paper form was, itself, an unusual thing. About the only time any Ellis group produced a hard copy of any kind was when it had to be distributed *outside* of Ellis: a media handout, say, or a quarterly stock report.

This was an *internal* report, but the subject was a hack they couldn't definitively source, and Max didn't want it living on a networked device, because he didn't know which systems had been compromised. This meant no emailing, or texting, or forwarding it as an attachment in a live Eyenet meeting, or any of the other electronic storage-and-distribution options that all would have otherwise made more sense than paper.

The report's data was gathered and collated on a non-networked laptop, and then exactly one copy was printed on a non-networked printer—this was a hard enough challenge that they nearly gave up and used a manual typewriter instead—after which that one copy was delivered, in person, to Max.

Nina Lambo was the author of the report, and her conclusion, after twenty-seven pages of dense text, was that she still didn't know the answer to the question the report had been produced to answer.

The question, which should not have been *that* difficult, was: who unlocked the file containing the *Aliens Are Talking to Us Now* press release of a week ago, and replaced some of the text with several rows of the word, "DANGER"?

Internally, only a handful of people knew about the draft press release at all, and after an exhaustive, down-to-the-keystroke review, each member of that handful was eliminated. (Max was one of them, because he insisted. Given he worked with approximately twenty-seven networked devices on any given week, his review took the longest.) Therefore, unless someone in the company knew something they shouldn't have known—and the security surrounding the release was tighter than the Pentagon's nuclear access codes—this was not a case of internal sabotage; it *had* to be an external hack.

But hacks leave traces behind. Some node, somewhere, had to have been compromised at a high enough security point to allow the hacker access to the EAS PR servers. There was a non-trivial amount of noise regarding the first part, because people tried to hack Ellis systems on the regular, albeit without getting far. But below that noise, there just wasn't any evidence of a penetration.

So, it wasn't internal sabotage and it wasn't an external hack. It was a third thing.

Nina had no idea what that third thing might be, but thought the *nature* of the alteration to the press release might yield clues.

"Consider," she wrote, "all the mischief someone capable of doing this *could* have committed. That they chose to do what they did instead clearly means something."

She then wrote another three paragraphs that could be summarized as, "but I don't know what."

Max tossed the report onto his desk and rubbed his eyes. This was going to bother him. A lot.

Then the phone rang, and everything changed all over again.

"CAN YOU REPEAT THAT?" Max said.

"Which part?" Mo asked. "The part where Sunset Station knows we've been lying to the world, or the part where I quit?"

"They're all *dead?*"

"The *aliens* are, yes."

"So it's been, what? On autopilot?"

"That's our best guess," Mo said.

"All right, well I don't care if Sunset Station knows what we've been saying," Max said. "That was bound to happen eventually. As long as they're up there and we're down here, we can control the messaging. We don't actually need them to be involved at all."

"You want to cut the team off from the planet entirely?"

"We can if we have to. No, the problem is, we need a new story now."

"Max, the problem is, we *made up the whole story*," Mo said. "You have to come clean, or this will just get worse."

"You can't quit, Mo."

"I can't stick around for what comes next either. I can't lie for you, and I will *not* lie to the crew in orbit."

"I'm not asking you to," Max said.

"Yeah, but you will," Mo said. "It's what's next. I don't know what that lie will be, but it won't matter because *whatever* it is, they won't believe it, and that's the problem. The crew's lives can depend on them believing what we say, and you've just introduced doubt into the conversation."

"Mo..."

"I'm a scientist, Max. So are all the people in that control room. So is everyone in orbit. Verifiably true things are very much life-and-death matters for us, especially with a team in space. I won't be a party any longer."

Max sighed. This was the problem with working with scientists; they thought empiricism governed *everything*, and not just certain corners of the shared reality.

"I don't accept your resignation," Max said. "Hand over your duties to Roman and take a few days off, and we'll have this conversation again when you're calmer."

"I'm perfectly calm, I..."

"Thanks for the update, Morris. Enjoy the break."

Max hung up. There were six dead aliens and a soon-to-be-dead mission commander to spin, and not a lot of time to figure out how to get it right. Mo would have to come to his senses on his own time.

Max sat back down at his desk and woke up the computer screen. He was at home, in an office he found himself using a lot more often these days. Ever since the alien ship's arrival, Max had been treated, in public, more like a head of state than a captain of industry. The crush of attention—which was always alarmingly high for a tech celebrity—more than doubled, and most of that attention was of the bad kind. For example, every publicized appearance he made was greeted by a large group of protestors. They never seemed to be protesting the same thing—even within the same protest group—and most of what they were accusing him of had nothing to do with anything he'd said or done. Also, every day brought a new, credible assassination threat. Unlike an *actual* head of state, Max didn't have a taxpayer-funded military force guarding his backside, so he had to rely on some very expensive private contractors instead.

Consequently, when he left his estate, it was under heavy guard, and in secret. And he hardly ever left his estate.

He toggled to the Ellis Direct Messaging app (they called it EDiM, because "EDM" meant something else to a large portion of the internet) and tagged Nina for a private. She responded "in 5" which said something pretty amazing about Nina Lambo; she was officially confident enough in her own role within the company to put the CEO on hold. Perhaps helping Max construct what she (privately) called the BFL—Big Fucking Lie—had emboldened her.

As he waited for her to join the private meeting, Max's eyes drifted to the top left corner of his screen. There, ever-present and therefore hardly even *seen* anymore—was the Ellis AI watermark. They put it on everything that had active AI running in the background, which was pitched as a courtesy but which was actually a legal loophole. According to the T&C everyone had to agree to in order to use an Ellis product, the watermark constituted both notification and consent.

Seeing it gave Max a crazy idea.

Nina entered the meeting, her face filling up the screen.

"Hi Max, sorry to keep you waiting," she said. "Is this about the report? Because we should really hold to protocol and do that on the landline."

"It's about Sunset Station," he said. "Something's happened up there, and the legend has to change. But first, I think I've figured out the third thing you were looking for."

KRIS

THERE WAS a full orchestra of warning beeps inside Kris's helmet. This had, perhaps, been going on for a while, so it was fair to say none of them was doing their job, which was to stir the helmet's owner into action.

Davina's voice did the trick, though.

"Kris, get the fuck up and get the fuck out of there," Dav said. Lovingly, somehow.

"Oh. Hi, Dav," Kris said. Kris was lying on her side, on the floor of the main room of the alien ship, deeply disliking the gravity but quite fond of not moving.

She'd been dreaming of aliens. Short, squat aliens with melting faces and ruptured eyeballs. Just before awakening, Kris discovered that she, too, was a short, squat alien with a melting face and a ruptured eyeball. It was possible that *this* was what actually woke her.

"Hi?" Dav said. "That's all you've got? Come on, soldier."

"Soldier. Right. Haven't been one of those for a while."

Kris pushed herself up to a sitting position. The room started spinning, so she didn't try going any further. Then she checked her gauges.

"Are you on your feet yet?" Dav said. "You've got to find the door, babe, so we can go get you."

"Not much point of that," Kris said. "I'm not being dramatic; just doing math. I've got less than an hour's worth of air left."

"I don't want to hear that."

"I don't want to *say* it. But it is what it is."

"You should have way more than that," Dav said. "It's a sensor malfunction."

Kris was looking at a reminder of the recent leak in her helmet glass: there was tape in her eyeline. When that had happened, she got an alert right away. None of the cacophony of alarms currently sounding off was for a suit leak.

"You make a good point," she said. "Hang on."

Kris grabbed the side of one of the stasis chambers/coffins and pulled herself to her feet, and then, slowly, awkwardly, slid the air tank off her back and set it on the floor. There was a gauge on the top that read the *actual* tank pressure; if it *was* a sensor malfunction, this was the way to find out.

"Ah," Kris said. "I see the problem. I have a leak; just not in the suit."

"Well, repair it!" Dav said.

"I'm doing it, I'm doing it, hang on."

She had to roll the tank around for a while before she found the pinhole leak. Like the helmet glass and the camera, the tank must have suffered from the impact with the tether cord.

(With all the damage it had done, she was beginning to wonder if she should be dead.)

Kris took the roll of tape from her belt and used a strip of it to seal the leak. By the time it was done, she only had forty-eight minutes of air left. But at least now it was an actual forty-eight minutes.

"It's sealed," Kris said. "For whatever good it'll do." She slid the tank onto her back again. "Think I'll take a look around."

"Kris...!"

"Davina, I either spend the last forty-eight minutes of my life failing to make it off the ship—to space, where there also isn't any air—or I spend it being the first human to explore an abandoned alien spaceship. It'd be nice if we could talk while I did that, but if that doesn't work for you, I'll open the line to Sandee instead."

There was a long enough silence that Kris wondered if Dav had chosen the second option. "What do you mean, abandoned?" Dav asked, eventually.

"There were six aliens aboard. They're all dead. It's just me in here."

"Dead how?"

"I'm guessing their stasis chambers malfunctioned," Kris said. "Unless they went in pre-desiccated."

"Or someone still on the ship killed them," Dav said.

"Yeah, I'm going to ignore that option."

"*How can I help?*" Susie chimed in.

"Oh. Hi, asshat," Kris said. "Unless you can find me some air, or an open door, you can't."

"*There is a doorway,*" Susie said, which was actually very helpful indeed.

"Uh. Okay, where?"

"Sorry, is she being helpful?" Davina asked. The "Susie" Kris was talking to had to be the local one in her suit, rather than the global version from the station. Otherwise, Dav would be able to hear both ends of the conversation.

"She said there's a doorway," Kris said. "So, maybe. Susie?"

"*How can I help?*"

"Where's that doorway?"

"*The doorway is in the wall!*"

"Okay but what wall?"

The wall at the far end of the room—if Kris's orientation was right, it was the end that went toward the nose of the ship—lit up in the infrared spectrum.

"Never mind," Kris said. "I think I see it. Davina, I'm heading for what should be the bridge, if this ship was built sensibly."

Dav grumbled something about going the wrong way, which Kris ignored.

Walking there (or anywhere) remained a sucky experience because of the gravity. Kris was clearly getting used to it—she no longer felt dizzy—but it was still rough. Then again, maybe she was being too hard on herself; returning astronauts generally got a week of bed rest before trying to lift anything heavier than a fork.

"What are you seeing?" Dav asked. "Describe the space."

"Darkness, mostly. I would love to find a normal light switch in this place, but it's only lit in infrared right now. Dimensions are, um, I don't know, twenty-five meters end to end. Ceiling is about... ah, no idea. Hang on."

She took out her flashlight, turned it on, and pointed it up. The beam definitely hit the ceiling, but it was impossible to tell how far it traveled when it did that, because shining a light up there evidently activated something else within the ship.

Kris was now looking at stars.

"Uh, wow. Okay. They've got themselves a moon roof. The aliens are face-up in their stasis chambers, so, ah, I guess they wanted a view? Otherwise, it doesn't make a ton of sense to have one."

"Are you saying a window has opened up on the roof of the ship?" Davina asked.

"Maybe. Not sure if it's two-way. Alan will have to send someone out to look later. Or whoever they put in charge."

"Don't talk like that."

"Right. How *is* Alan?"

"We have him. He'll be fine. Worry about yourself."

Kris stopped at a glowing rectangle in the wall. She studied the space where an access panel should by all rights be located, but there was nothing there.

"Okay, Susie lied," she said. "I asked for a doorway; she pointed me to a door I don't know how to open."

"Try 'open sesame,'" Dav said.

"Funny," Kris said, then decided it was worth a try. "Open door," she said.

And then the door slid open.

"Dav, you're not gonna believe this."

"Don't tell me it worked."

"Okay, but it worked. I know it sounds crazy, but this ship just responded to a vocal command. Like, *Star Trek* shit."

"Your helmet's still on, right?" Dav asked.

"It is, yes."

"How did the ship hear you?"

This was a good question. Even if there was an atmosphere to carry the sound, as long as Kris had her helmet on nothing she said would have been audible *outside* of her helmet.

Either the alien ship had tapped into her comms, or the door opening at that moment was a coincidence.

Or—and this was probably it—there was a sensor that detected someone standing there.

"I probably just tripped a sensor," Kris said.

"That makes more sense."

Kris poked her head through the doorway. It was dark on the other side, of course, because everything on this ship was dark. When no obvious threats presented, she crossed the threshold, and the bridge lit up, albeit only in infrared.

There was a large, concave control panel at the far end of

the room, surrounding a chair, no windows, no other exits, and no other places to sit. It reminded her (of all things) of a high-end gaming console.

The panel displayed a complex series of swirls and whorls in a style she'd come to identify as text in the alien language. But unlike a nominally sane control panel—in which one might expect the words to directly correspond to a specific button or switch, and describe said button or switch's function—this text was *moving*.

"Yeah, okay," Kris said. "I found the cockpit. Kinda."

"Describe it for me?" Davina asked.

"No window, no wheel, a chair..."

"*There is air now*," Susie interrupted.

"What else?" Dav asked.

"Hang on, Dav. Susie, what did you say?"

"*How can I help?*"

"Susie, you just said there's air," Kris said.

"*Kris Standard asked for air, and a door. There is air, and a door.*"

"*What's* she saying?" Davina asked.

"She said I have air."

"Ah, okay. Kris, I don't, I don't think you should listen to her. Remember... I mean, let's be careful, huh?"

Davina was trying to bring up, tactfully, Kris's evident proclivity for aural hallucination, given what happened the last time she was stranded. That Kris did not think of her previous experience as a hallucination at all was suddenly relevant.

"You don't think I should trust her?" Kris asked.

"It's asshat, babe. No, I don't think you should trust her."

There was a sensor on Kris's suit that, in theory, should be capable of notifying her when the room she was in had breathable atmosphere, and it was therefore okay to remove her helmet. The tech team implied that this sensor would work everywhere; in other words, should they take the suit into a place that was somewhere *other* than the Ellis Space Station or an Ellis shuttle, that it would still perform this task, thanks to some internal detection system. However, Kris had long suspected that the suit was actually just reporting back what the airlock was telling it. In short, since she wasn't standing inside of something built by Ellis, the information being reported by the suit at this moment—that there was *not* breathable air outside of her helmet—could *also* not be trusted.

She did not relay this bit of logic to Davina, who sounded alarmed enough already.

"Copy that," Kris said. "I'll keep the helmet on, for now."

"For *now*? Kris..."

"Dav, in a half an hour I'm either *definitely* suffocating, or only *probably* suffocating. Right? I may as well go out having tried. In the meantime, I'm gonna sit in this chair and see what happens."

Kris shuffled to the front of the chair, and sat. Immediately, the chair adjusted underneath her, to accommodate her physique: the seat narrowed, the armrests lowered and widened, and the entire thing lifted her to within arm's reach of the console.

"Wow. That was cool."

"Kris?" Davina said, way louder than she needed to. "Kris are you okay??"

"I'm... as okay as I was a minute ago. Why?"

"I think you woke up the ship," she said.

SANDEE

ALAN WAS BACK aboard the station. Paul had him in their makeshift sick bay (the break room, because Ellis Aero never saw fit to create a space to convalesce from injuries) and was still trying to get Alan's suit off, without Alan's help: he was still unconscious. Alan's right arm was definitely broken, but the head injury was the biggest concern of the moment.

Davina and Josip were still on the shuttle. As soon as Alan was off-loaded, they took the shuttle back out, and were hurrying over to the alien ship. Their intent was to be reasonably nearby when Kris made it back outside, so as to rescue her. This was definitely wishful thinking; even the most optimistic timeline had them in position thirty minutes *after* Kris was out of oxygen. But they had to try.

Dav was still on active comms with Kris. Sandee was recording it for posterity, on the assumption Kris's description of the alien ship would be of value later... and also, to preserve Kris Standard's last words. Which was awful to contemplate.

It was about a minute after the shuttle relaunched that the alien ship lit up, which was fantastic timing as far as Sandee was concerned, because her adrenaline had just begun to crash. She needed something new and terrifying to keep going.

"The ship's awake, y'all," she said, to nobody in particular. "Jesus Christ, the ship's awake."

The ship always had *some* visible-spectrum lighting going on, or rather, it did once it took off that cloaking tech that kept it transparent. The lighting had been of the non-direct sort, coming from embedded sources just at the surface, that shone sideways along the hull. But it wasn't a whole *lot* of light; just enough to describe the ship's dimensions.

What was happening *now* looked very different: long, white lines ran down the hull, stretching from the nose to the tail; the rear rockets (previously a black hole of nothing) now had a dim red glow; spotlights (landing lights, perhaps) arced from below; and bulbs that could be headlights beamed from above and around the antennas and/or weapons array jutting out of the nose cone.

Watching it happen reminded Sandee of what a computer screen looked like when it was toggled awake.

"Davina," Sandee said, opening a private line, "do you see?"

"Yeah, Kris did that," Davina said. "She reached the cockpit."

"Well tell her to stop touching shit," Sandee said. "Giving me a heart attack over here."

"Touching shit's the only way she gets the airlock door open," Dav said.

"All right well, make sure she doesn't fire a rocket or whatever."

"If you think it'd help. Not sure she's taking any advice today."

"Please."

The line to Monterrey flashed. Given the time of day, they didn't have eyes on the ship yet, but they might've seen Sandee's vitals jump. She was about to open their line for an update, when a different screen flashed. This one was for the program that was collating all the information it could find on Ellis Aero's big lie. Sandee had no idea how Susie managed to gain un-firewalled access to the global internet, but was pretty sure it wouldn't last; the best thing to do, then, was to save off everything as fast as possible so she could go through it later.

The program was prioritizing *new* information, and high-value information directly sourced from Ellis Aero and the EAS PR team. It was flashing because something that was both new and red-flagged as high value had just been identified.

Curious, Sandee opened up the file.

"What the hell?" she muttered, as she read through it.

She was looking at a transcript of a conversation between Max Ellis and Morris Esteban, from no more than ten minutes ago.

There was no way either one of these guys would have committed to a recording or transcription, given what they were talking about. And after that, there was no way they would have made that transcription available to discovery on the internet.

This should not exist, she thought.

"Hey, Susie?"

"How can I help?"

"Yeah, can you tell me where this file came from?"

"I don't understand the question!" Susie said.

Susie said this all the time. Her program appeared to prioritize not understanding things. Usually, the questioner gave up, assuming what was being asked was, A: outside Susie's realm of knowledge (almost everything, it seemed), B: phrased in a way Susie couldn't understand, or C: posed after too long of a pause. Susie had almost no conversational short-term memory, so if you didn't ask her a follow-up question immediately, you had to go back to the beginning. That this made her effectively useless in longer interactions didn't seem to bother any of her programmers.

Sandee had been hearing, "I don't understand the question" from Susie for a while now. But this was the first time she considered an option D: Susie was lying to her.

"I'll rephrase," Sandee said. "Susie?"

"How can I help?"

"The file on my computer appears to be a real-time transcription of a private conversation that neither party would have recorded. Can you explain how it *was* recorded, and how it ended up on my computer?"

The ensuing pause was lengthy enough that Sandee thought she had perhaps gotten through.

"I don't understand the question!" Susie said again. Sandee was about to try a third time, when Susie, quite unexpectedly, elaborated.

"Astronaut Sandee Fellowes tasked the enhanced search bot to locate all mentions of Sunset Station's alien contacts, prioritized by recency and proximity to source. The transcript in question satisfies those search metrics."

"But this transcript shouldn't exist," Sandee said. "This was a private conversation. How did you, or, how did the search bot that's a *part* of you, get this?"

"I don't understand the question!" Susie said again.

Dammit, she thought. Sometimes, talking to Susie was like asking a confused three-year old why she had blood on her shoes. Yes, she has shoes, yes there's blood. Where did the blood come from? From the shoe, obviously. *I don't understand the question.*

The most benign explanation for this transcript's existence was that either Max or Morris *did* record it, intentionally, using one of Ellis's everywhere-all-the-time AI transcription bots.

(Sandee didn't trust transcription bots, and disabled them

whenever she could figure out how. The first time she used one, in a meeting, she discovered the bot didn't record anything she—the only person of color on the call—said. The technology had improved somewhat since, but the distrust never went away.)

Whoever authorized the transcription would then have had to deposit the text in a searchable place that was not behind a security firewall. Sandee assumed that to be so because she didn't think the enhanced search bot she'd engaged was capable of *hacking*; it was just scraping the internet.

The first part—a secret recording—seemed possible. But not the second. No way it would be stored somewhere that was easily discoverable.

Then Sandee had a terrible thought.

"Susie?"

"How can I help?"

"Are you in communication with other bots? Say, a bot at mission control?"

"Of course!"

"Of course, of course. Great. Another question."

"How can I help?"

"Susie, do you and the bots on the surface listen and transcribe *by default?*"

Susie didn't say she failed to understand this time. She didn't say *anything*, for about five seconds. Then:

"The Source listens to everything."

And then, all of Sandee's comm lines went dark at the same time.

KRIS

KRIS WAS afraid to touch anything.

According to Davina, just by sitting in the chair, Kris had activated the ship's external lighting, which was—surprisingly—not exclusively in infrared, as everything inside the ship appeared to be.

"I guess that makes sense," she said.

"What's that?" Davina asked. "What makes sense?"

"I'm just thinking aloud, sorry. It makes sense that the external lights would encompass a wider range of the spectrum. They want to be seen, and not just by creatures with their own optical range. But *in* the ship, it's all built for just their eyeballs."

"And the writing on the outside is for their eyes only," Dav added.

"Exactly."

But the *chair* had adjusted to Kris when she sat in it, which made her wonder if she could get the interior lighting to make the same accommodation.

The chair knew to change because it interacted with my ass, she thought. *How do I interact with this panel* optically?

To see if it would make any difference in the display, Kris

lifted the infrared screen on the helmet. As expected, she could no longer view the lights on the console.

She waited, to see if that changed. It did not.

"I can't see anything," she muttered. Then, on thinking about it, she said it louder: "I can't see anything. My eyes can't see infrared."

"What are you doing?" Davina asked.

"The ship can hear me, right? I'm testing a theory."

"We don't know that."

"All right, I'm testing *two* theories."

"*How can I help?*" Susie asked.

"Hi, Susie," Kris said. "I don't think you can help me with this one."

"*Kris Standard's eyes cannot see in the infrared range,*" Susie said. "*Infrared is outside the range of the human visible spectrum.*"

"Uh. Yes. That's right."

Susie the Support Bot was sounding incredibly competent all of a sudden.

Equally suddenly, and considerably more alarming, the panel's lighting changed from infrared to a dull—but visible—fire-engine red. It was just as indecipherable as ever, but now Kris didn't have to have the infrared screen down on her helmet to look at it.

Kris stood and looked around the room. The running lights on the ceiling and the doorframe were also perfectly visible now.

Kris had a wild thought. "Susie, did *you* do that?"

"*How can I help?*" Susie asked.

"Did you fix the lights?"

"*I don't understand the question!*"

"Never mind. Hey, Davina?"

"What is it?"

"Check your local Susie. Mine's suddenly a lot smarter than she should be."

The ask was followed by a lengthy silence on Davina's end.

"Don't take off your helmet," Dav said.

"What? No, this isn't about that. I mean... well, no, actually I guess it *is* about that."

"Kris!"

"I asked for a door and then there was a door. I complained that I couldn't see infrared, and now the lights in here are in the visible range. I asked for *air*..."

"None of that had anything to do with Susie, Kris. It's wishful thinking. Your oxygen's getting low and affecting..."

"What if it's not wishful thinking? What if Susie is controlling this ship, somehow?"

"That's insane. We both know she's not that advanced."

"Think back to when we were trying to figure out how to get into this ship's airlock," Kris said. "It didn't *just* open; we told Susie what we wanted and she told *us* it was open."

"Correlation doesn't equal causation, babe, come on. Now why don't you see about using that control panel to get the airlock door to open, and we'll get you some oxygen before it's too late."

"I can't *read* the panel," Kris said. "It's in alien. And I'm not going to just start pressing random buttons and hoping for the best. We can agree that's a bad idea, right?"

"*How can I help?*" Susie asked.

"Hi, Susie, can you teach me how to read alien?"

"*I don't understand the question!*" Susie said.

"Worth a shot."

"What is she saying?" Davina asked.

"Nothing important. Look, no matter what I do in the next few minutes you're not going to have enough... hold on."

The display on the main console blinked a couple of times, and then the symbols changed.

Kris stepped up to the panel to get a closer look. The whorls and swirls had been replaced by slightly more familiar symbols.

"Hey, Dav, you're not gonna believe this."

"I can almost guarantee you're correct," Davina said. "What is it?"

"I don't have to learn how to read alien anymore. But I *am* going to need a crash course in Chinese."

DAVINA

IT WAS a good thing Josip was there to fly the shuttle, because Davina was having a lot of trouble concentrating on anything other than Kris.

They could only push the shuttle so hard—come in too hot and they wouldn't have a chance to brake before reaching the hull. They were relying on a back-of-the-envelope calculation to figure out how fast they could go and for how long before they started slowing down, tweaking the math several times to come up with the ideal calculation, the one that delivered them there the fastest with the most acceptable risk.

The problem was that every version of their calculations got them there much too late. Even if Kris was waiting inside the airlock, she'd have had to hold her breath for about twenty minutes to have a chance. Knowing this, Davina was inclined to push the shuttle past the upper limit of that calculation, even knowing it would likely turn them into a metallic gray splotch on the side of the alien ship.

So, Jo flew the shuttle.

Not that either approach much mattered, because aside from the holding-her-breath-twenty-minutes issue, Kris wasn't even in the airlock. (And she couldn't open the outer door even if she was.) No, Kris was on the ship's bridge, having something that sounded a lot like a psychotic break.

"What do you mean, Chinese?" Davina asked, then added, "literally, Chinese?"

"Yes, literally," Kris said. "The dashboard isn't showing the alien runes anymore. It's, it *really* looks like Chinese characters. Maybe it's not, but that's what I'm seeing."

You also heard Susie tell you to take off your helmet, Davina thought.

"Where's your oxygen at?" Dav asked.

"You think this is hypoxia talking?"

"I think you should consider it."

"I still have seven minutes left," Kris said. "I'm going to try to..."

The line went dead.

"Kris?" Davina half-shouted. "Kris??"

The shuttle lurched abruptly, pulling her forward in her seat. They were slowing down, for some reason. She looked up to the front of the cockpit, where Josip, unbelted, was manipulating the controls as quickly as it was possible to do in zero gravity.

"Jo, why are we *braking*?" she asked.

He didn't respond. They both had helmets on, in anticipation of one or both of them needing to leave the shuttle quickly, so all their one-to-one communication was being routed through the shuttle's system. When talking, she usually heard a *click* at the end of whatever she said—a subtle indication the words had been sent—that was now absent.

Josip couldn't hear her.

She unbelted and floated to the front of the shuttle. Were he to reengage the engines at that moment she'd have been catapulted into the back of the room, but since the shuttle's boosters weren't *all* that powerful, she'd probably be fine.

She got up behind him and said his name again. When this didn't work, she checked the atmospheric readings in the suit to confirm that they still had breathable air, and took the helmet off, lashed it to the side of a chair, and touched Jo on the arm.

He jumped back in surprise, and said something Polish and swear-y that she couldn't hear. She pantomimed him removing his helmet, which he did.

"I just lost Kris," Davina said. "And internal comms are down. What's happening here?"

"We have begun to slow, only I have nothing to do with it," he said. "Our deceleration was not scheduled for another twenty minutes."

Davina looked at the settings on the control panel. "We're braking too hard; we'll be dead in space a thousand feet from the hull."

"I know, but I can't get the reverse thrusters to disengage."

Davina switched her comms to the link with the hub. "Sandee, we're having some problems with the shuttle."

No answer, aside from plenty of static.

"Sandee, this is the shuttle. Can you hear us?"

Nothing. Josip toggled to another channel.

"Monterrey, this is Josip in the shuttle, are you receiving this? Over."

More silence.

"Well," he said, "at least we have not lost *all* power this time."

MAX

MAX ELLIS'S entire life was an ongoing work of creative fiction. Which was another way of saying about three-quarters of what everyone *thought* was true about the man was not, by any objective measure, *actually* true.

This was deliberate. He had been curating fictitious elements of his own life since he was a child, and had yet to run into a situation in which doing so ended up being a detriment. (That is, a detriment to *him*, which was the only metric that mattered.)

Max was often referred to as a "self-made man" which, to a certain degree was definitely true: he created "Max Ellis," a person who legally did not exist *before* being created. This was not what people generally meant when describing someone—almost exclusively the extremely wealthy—"self-made." In *that* context, it meant, "look at this billionaire, he/she started from nothing!" Max didn't start from nothing, but didn't correct anyone who claimed otherwise.

Before Max Ellis was Max Ellis, he was Leopold Drucker. Leopold's great grandfather, Adelbert Drucker, was a German shipping magnate who may or may not have made a fortune shipping heavy freight in support of the Nazi military apparatus. (A historian would say he did. But the first ten hits in an online search would say he did not. Was this peculiar? Yes, yes it was.) Adelbert's son, Leopold's grandfather Carl, emigrated to the U.S. after the fall of the Third Reich—more accurately, *during* the fall of the Third Reich—with his family's substantial holdings, in gold, which Carl converted into a chain of shoe stores along the East coast.

Then Carl had a son named Frederick, and Frederick had a son named Leopold, and Leopold looked over the family history and decided everything—his name, his lineage, all but the not-insubstantial *wealth* that came from being a Drucker—had to go. And so, he became Max Ellis, grandson of a Pennsylvania coal miner and son of a dentist, who started from nothing.

Which was not true.

What was *almost* true was that he left home with nothing more than the clothes on his back; almost, because in addition to the clothing on his back, he also had about five million dollars in his pocket. What he did with that five million was pretty impressive, inasmuch as he turned it into a personal fortune measured in hundreds of billions. It could well be said that *this* part (the millions to billions) qualified him as "self-made." The problem was that nobody really knew how easy or hard doing that might be, because very, very few people got a chance to start with five million in the first place.

Anyway. The point was that Max Ellis's life was built upon a core fiction, and fiction was how it proceeded from there.

Max's first business venture took place in a small corner of the internet devoted to horoscopes and general fortune-telling, with a cash-starved startup called Psychic Central.

The young programmers behind Psychic Central were trying to connect online users with online psychics, with the twist being that they planned to not use any actual psychics (if it could be said that there was such a thing as an actual psychic.) Instead, they were developing an algorithm that could do approximately the same thing.

Only—and this was the part that made no sense to Max—they planned to keep the existence of the algorithm a secret.

That was all wrong; the appeal of the service was the novelty of the algo, especially once they got over their pedantry and called it AI.

It *wasn't* AI. It was—and the company's founders kept repeating this, because for some reason they thought Max hadn't heard them the first fifteen times they said so—just an algorithm. They were willing to go as far as calling it "machine learning," but it wasn't artificial intelligence any more than a spreadsheet was artificial intelligence.

Every time, Max would calmly tell them they were entirely missing the point. The point was this: more people would want to use it if they *knew* it was a computer on the other end.

What's more, not only did it not have to be real AI, it didn't even have to be a working algorithm—which was actually fantastic, because when Max bought the company, the algo didn't work yet, and the reason it didn't work was because they needed more input data—to teach it—than they could afford to buy.

And here was where Max's particular business approach—which boiled down to, "keep lying until it's not a lie"—really showed out.

Max bought ten thousand horoscopes from a newspaper chain that had no use for old horoscopes. (*No surprise the news industry is dying*, he thought at the time. *They don't even understand the value of what they already own.*) Then he handed the horoscopes to the programmers, told them to remove any sign-specific references—Taurus, Leo, etc.—and set the horoscopes up in a simple randomizer. Next, he told the programmers to work out what data points they needed to have in order to train their algorithm.

From there, it was easy. A new user to the site—now rebranded as Psychic Robot—would create an account, answer ten decently personal questions, and then get a psychic reading. The answers to the questions went to train the algo, and the reading was pulled, at random, from the pile of old horoscopes.

Nobody aside from Max thought this would work. They were wrong; not only did it work, the site was such an enormous success that the founders soon had more than enough data to train their algorithm.

Finally having a functioning algo turned out to be unfortunate for the future of the company, because nobody liked the algorithm's output as much as they did the random, denatured horoscope readings. Psychic Robot ran as intended for only three days, before Max ordered them to switch it back. He gave the programmers another month to tweak their algorithm, but even before they came back with an updated version, he'd reached the conclusion that they would never get to where they had to be for the project to work.

And so, unwilling to wait for everyone to get tired of the horoscopes, and disinterested in plugging the algorithm back in and watching the user base bleed off, Max decided to go out on top: overnight, shockingly, Psychic Robot disappeared from the internet.

When asked what happened, Max hinted darkly that the AI had gotten too good, too fast, and that *certain government agencies* had an active interest in seeing it discontinued. Then he promised that "they" hadn't heard the last of him, and that his next AI project would be even more impressive.

Thus began the legend of the man calling himself Max Ellis.

As for his original investment in the company, even after closing it all down and buying out the contracts of the employees, Max came out ahead. Within days of the closure, he accepted an offer to sell all of the data Psychic Robot had collected on its users, for three times what he'd paid to buy the company in the first place.

THERE HAD BEEN over a dozen AI launches since, under the corporate Ellis AI umbrella. All of them—from Susie the Support Bot to the AI that "drove" the Ellis Auto, to the various social media, advertising, search engine, business support, writing and email bots—were, fundamentally, exactly as real as Psychic Robot.

This wasn't precisely a secret, not in the way "we made up the whole thing about the aliens talking to Sunset Station" was a secret. But everyone liked the idea that the various AI bots they were using were *actual* discrete, self-aware intelligences (rather than digital parrots) so much, people just accepted the lie.

What *was* an actual secret, was that every single seemingly independent AI model within the Ellis corporate sphere was actually the *same* AI. (There was no official name for it, since it was a secret, but unofficially, the engineers called it Maximum AI. Max for short.)

This was Max Ellis's big gamble. As it was in the Psychic Robot days, so it was now: the only way to develop a real, all-purpose AI was to first collect a simply *massive* amount of feedback data. Which was why every one of the AI models, from Susie on down, was secretly networked to a single hub that lived on a server farm in rural Nebraska.

The hope was that this hive mind AI would eventually figure out how to problem-solve by cross-communicating solutions. That is, perhaps a challenge to Bobby the Business

Support Bot could be worked out by looking at a solution to a similar problem discovered by Annie the Advertising Bot.

The last time Max checked, Maximum AI had not yet bridged this gap, or given any other indication of what might qualify as true independent thought. However, it *had* been a while since he'd gotten an update from the team. (Or from any team, outside of Ellis Aero and EAS PR.) Perhaps there had been a change.

According to Nina Lambo, nobody—more specifically, no *person*—from in or outside the company had altered the press release. But Maximum AI was not a person. And, Maximum AI was plugged into every last network in the Ellis empire, whether those networks were fully aware of that fact or not.

Maximum AI could *absolutely* have done it.

As to *why* it would do something like that...? Well, that was a different question. Max was working with *if, how,* and *when*; he'd have to get to *why* later.

It took an hour to set up a call with Stanton Tollhouse, the head of Ellis AI, because Max wanted them to talk over low-tech landlines rather than any of the normal channels, and that wasn't easy work out on Stanton's end.

"That's... I'm sorry, say that again?" Stanton asked, once Max finally got him on the phone. "You think Maximum's become conscious?"

"It's what makes the most sense," Max said.

"Except it doesn't make *any* sense. Don't you have more important shit to worry about right now?"

Stanton Tollhouse was a trust fund baby Max plucked from Harvard the day he graduated. He was an arrogant jackass who thought he was always right. Annoyingly, the arrogance wasn't entirely unwarranted, because so far it had turned out he *was* always right. It was one of the reasons Max hired him.

Not the main one, though. Stanton Tollhouse was also

actively terrified that truly sentient AI might someday exist. He swore, often, that the day he became convinced Maximum AI was *alive* was the day he would personally take an axe to the servers. Whether or not he would actually *do* this wasn't the point. (Although, keeping a guy around who was willing to swing an axe if the circumstance warranted did seem prudent.) The point was, Stanton had exceedingly high standards when testing for sentience; he was not about to be misled by his own wishful thinking, because he very much did not wish for it to be so.

"I do have a lot to worry about, Stanton," Max agreed. "So the fact that I'm worrying about *this,* right now, should have your attention."

"You're right; you've got it. Tell me why you're asking."

Max did, omitting a couple of details, such as that the press release that was replaced by repetitions of "danger" was an internally created fiction.

"It's an interesting thought, man," Stanton said. "But it's about as likely the printer you used became self-aware. No way Maximum could've done that."

"You're *sure?*"

"Am I sure without *checking?* No, but I'm not sure of anything without checking. I hold a mirror to my face every morning to make sure I'm still fucking breathing. But you're talking about a *leap*, Max. This is *way* beyond *je pense donc je suis*, you hear me?"

"I get it. Check anyway."

"You're the boss. I'll order a full diagnostic. Give me a couple of hours. But don't get your hopes up. And maybe check that printer too, huh?"

MERRITT

THERE WAS something very wrong with Ellis Social.

Merritt Zass had been arguing that very point for *years*, both online and IRL, so for them to make this observation *now* was hardly a glass-shattering event. They were, in fact, one of the most prominent of voices on the subject of how very much was wrong with the Ellis global empire writ large—mostly under the Ellis Social handle NoMerit17, but sometimes as themselves, on podcasts and the occasional news standup. They had not yet managed to parlay their role as professional skeptic into a full-time gig (watching someone throw rocks at the largest tech conglomerate in the world was still very niche) but they enjoyed a minor celebrity status nonetheless.

What made *this* observation—that something was wrong with Ellis Social—different from the other ones was that Merritt was pretty sure what they were seeing wasn't an *intentional* act on the part of the ES team. Specifically, the bots were being nice to Merritt, and there was no way anyone at Ellis Social tasked the bots to do that.

IT WAS an unfortunate irony that the very best place to call attention to the latest Ellis malfeasance was on the world's largest social media app, Ellis Social. This was one of the most common complaints lodged against Merritt's investigative work. Not, "your logic is unsound," or, "you may be paranoid," but, "if you hate them so much, don't use their products." But there was simply no other way to reach a large enough audience to make what Merritt was doing worth the time they put into it.

Ellis Social could, of course, shut Merritt down any time, except that doing so would unquestionably draw more attention to their work than it would have otherwise gotten. So what ES did instead, was target Merritt with their bots.

This had been going on for years. Merritt would write an article about how the Ellis's Rover AI wasn't actually driving the cars, and within seconds of sharing, the article would be inundated with pro-Rover attestations (which wasn't too bad) and personal attacks (which could get pretty bad.) They were so *obviously* bot-produced posts from bot-created accounts that, to save time, Merritt added a subroutine to all their ES interactions, automatically replying to each bot post with: "this is a bot".

These bots were also, just as obviously, acting under the direction of a person or team at Ellis Media. Ellis denied it, but nobody took the denials seriously. (Probably. It was definitely true that nobody in Merritt's orbit took the denials seriously, but Merritt willing to consider that they existed in an information bubble in that regard.)

The bots really kicked into overdrive after the Ellis Aero news that the aliens had established contact with the Ellis Space Station. Merritt was not the first, or only, person to call bullshit on this—Merritt was pretty sure they had the head of NASA in their corner—but Merritt might have gotten the worst blowback of any of them. A few hours after Merritt posted their first piece (title: "*Sure*, the Aliens Are Having Tea with Kris Standard, and I'm Fucking Max Ellis.") their account was suspended for two days, under a dubious standards violation. When Merritt got back on, they discovered that the post had been buried under so much bot criticism it was nearly impossible to find the original piece.

Merritt wrote another post, and another, and another. All were variations on the same theme: Max Ellis was the very last person we should trust to tell us the truth about the aliens, and if you think otherwise you're either very, very gullible, or you're on his payroll.

The bot bombardments continued, until... well, this was where things started to get weird.

Merritt's last piece, "Pic or It's Not True," got hit with the usual wave of artificial indignation, at *first*. But then, the bots started *agreeing* with it.

So true, and you're right to say it! said one.

Ellis is lying and we need the truth! said another.

Doxx the aliens, read a third. (This didn't make sense, but the bots only occasionally *did* make sense. For the most part, they functioned by smashing incendiary words together in a semblance of proper sentence structure.)

On and on these posts came, all from accounts that were very clearly bots, *Ellis* bots, and all agreeing that the man behind the curtain was lying to the world, and "we" should do something about it.

Merritt could only come up with one explanation. It was a *crazy* explanation, but whatever.

They opened up a window for a new post.

Holy Shit, Someone Hacked the Ellis Bots, they wrote.

KRIS

"DAVINA??" Kris shouted. There had been a burst of static on the line, and now Dav wasn't answering. "Dav, are you okay?"

Her mind went to the worst possible conclusion first, which was that something catastrophic had happened to the shuttle. But when Kris tried Sandee, she didn't answer either. Possibly, something had happened to both the shuttle and the ESS at the same time, but there was a more benign conclusion: *they* were fine, and it was Kris's comms that were malfunctioning.

This led her to actually go through all the warning notifications sounding off in her helmet, which just meant setting them to *ignore* until later (with "later" being well after Kris expected to no longer be alive) one at a time, in order to open up the diagnostic on her communications menu.

According to that menu, Kris was in fact both sending and receiving audio.

"Hey, Susie?" she asked.

"How can I help?"

"Are you in contact with the hub or the shuttle? Are they okay?"

"Which question would you like me to answer?"

Susie was getting snarky. Which was probably inevitable given she was being trained on feedback from a team of extremely snarky individuals.

"I'd like you to answer both," Kris said.

"Ellis Space Station and the remote shuttle are intact," Susie said. *"One team member is being treated for a broken bone and a concussion, and there are multiple elevated heartrates. Would you like for me to provide you with more details on their health statuses?"*

"Thank you, no. That was, uh, surprisingly comprehensive. Are you in contact with them?"

"I am monitoring their health."

Did she always do that? Kris wondered.

"But are you in *contact* with them?" Kris asked. "Can you speak to them?"

"Communications have been suspended," Susie said.

"Sorry, what?"

"Communications have been suspended," Susie repeated, like this was the most normal thing ever.

"How? By whom? What are you talking about?"

"Which question would you like me to answer first?"

"Christ, okay. Um. Susie."

"How can I help?"

"I would like to speak to Davina and Sandee directly. Can you help me do that?"

"Communications have been suspended."

"Can you override the suspension?"

"Communications cannot be overridden, as communications have been suspended."

"Susie."

"How can I help?"

"Did *you* suspend communications?"

"*Communications were not suspended by Susie the Support Bot.*"

"You're referring to yourself in third person now?"

"*Susie the Support Bot is...*"

"Yes, I know," Kris interrupted.

A more urgent alarm started sounding off in Kris's helmet. This was the one reporting how much oxygen she had left, and it wasn't a lot.

"Look, Susie."

"*How can I help?*"

"You can let me talk to Davina again," Kris said. "That's how you can help."

"*Communications have been suspended.*"

"I don't care, Susie. I don't know what protocol you think you're following right now, but I'm going to be dead in five minutes, so I'd very much like to say my goodbyes."

Susie didn't answer for a beat, which gave Kris some irrational hope that the bot was doing as Kris requested.

"*Kris Standard does not have any current medical risks. Kris Standard should expect remain alive for a period of longer than five minutes.*"

"Did you *look* at my oxygen gauge?" Kris asked.

"*Kris Standard has air.*"

"Five minutes' worth!"

"*Kris Standard has air. There is air.*"

There was no point in arguing, both because Susie was evidently malfunctioning at the moment and because arguing with her was about as effective as shouting at a word processing program.

The question was, how *much* malfunctioning was Susie actually doing right now? Was her insistence that there was breathable air on the alien ship another aspect of a malfunction?

It doesn't matter, Kris thought. *I either suffocate with the helmet on or with the helmet off.*

I just thought I'd have a little more time.

"All right, Susie," she said.

"How can I help?"

"If I die, you can tell Davina I was thinking of her. Can you do that?"

"That depends on when Kris Standard dies." Susie said. *"Would you like to access actuarial tables? According to..."*

"No, just. Never mind."

"Of course!"

Kris took two deep breaths, held the second one, and flipped the latch under her chin. The suit, which was operating under the reasonable assumption that it was currently being used in outer space, set off a cacophony of warning signals designed to either wake up or deafen the astronaut inside of it.

She ignored the alarms and kept going, flipping the latch on the back of her neck and then twisting the helmet to the left until she heard the hiss of air escaping.

Closing her eyes (she had no reason to do this, but did it anyway) she lifted the helmet off of her head.

The room wasn't cold. That was the first thing she noticed: not cold, but temperate. This didn't necessarily mean *much*, because places without atmosphere (such as outer space) also didn't feel cold, or hot or anything; like sound, temperature needed a medium to travel through. But she still felt a tiny bit better about her odds, because it didn't *feel* like nothing.

She opened her eyes, which neither froze in their sockets nor exploded. And then, she exhaled the air from her lungs, and tried taking in a breath.

There was indeed atmosphere. And, given her lungs were not actively screaming at her, that atmosphere included oxygen.

She would not be dying in the next five minutes.

Amazed, Kris put the helmet down on the chair and walked around the room, looking at everything with unfiltered eyes.

Was it like this on the whole ship? Or just the bridge? It seemed unlikely that the beings who made the ship just happened to also be oxygen-breathers, but the alternative was that the *ship* adjusted the atmosphere for Kris, which seemed even less likely.

Kris fumbled around her neck for a small earpiece-and-microphone setup she'd have to use if she wanted to interact with her spacesuit without the helmet on. After slipping off the head sock to get to her ear (and hearing a chime to indicate it was live) she said, "Susie? Can you hear me?"

"*How can I help?*" Susie said.

The bot's answer didn't come from the earpiece; it came from the alien ship.

Stunned, Kris pulled the earpiece out, and said, "Susie, how long have you been aboard this ship?"

STANTON

"I'M GOING to need my axe," Stanton Tollhouse said, to the deeply confused intern who'd unfortunately been tasked with assisting the project head, during what was supposed to be an easy shift.

The intern's name was either Lois or Louis, and Stanton had no patience to learn which was right—their gender was not a useful indicator here, as this was not obvious by looking at them and Stanton had had enough run-ins with the HR department to know not to ask—so he just referred to them as Lo and hoped everybody thought it was a charming nickname.

"Is that a *Lord of the Rings* reference?" Lo asked. This was a stupid question that demonstrated exactly why Stanton very much did not want to have an intern assisting him at this time.

"Why would you think that? No, I mean I need for you to go down the hall, go into my office, and fetch my axe."

They were standing in the computer center that supported the Maximum AI servers: fifteen terminals, all actively running one thing or another. There were no humans other than Stanton and Lois/Louis in sight, because the maintenance of this, the most complex artificial intelligence program on the planet, was almost fully automated.

The decision to make it (almost) fully automated was not Stanton's. He was firmly against it, but when asked to explain why, all he could muster was, "because Skynet", which nobody else found compelling. His concerns were routinely dismissed *anyway,* as everyone who knew him at all eventually decided what they called his "alarmist tendencies" were part of a bit, wherein he was the perpetual curmudgeon who would always introduce the absolute worst thing that could happen in every scenario. He *did* tend do that, but not because—as Max Ellis himself seemed to think—he wanted to make sure the worst-case scenario was at least given voice. No, when he said he thought a thing could happen, it was because he really thought it could happen and that, in happening, it would be really, really, incredibly bad for everybody.

Stanton wanted the first line of server support to be human, because even though that would be both less efficient and more expensive, humans wouldn't collaborate with the other humans to make it look like something that was happening was *not* happening, or vice versa. Whereas a single computer system, however independent it might be from the system it was supporting, could absolutely do something like that.

Stanton lost that argument, just like he lost almost every other argument he'd made for inserting inefficiencies into the process in the service of not creating a single-point-of-failure computer overlord. He would have quit by now, except he didn't trust anyone who might take his place, and also Max seemed to genuinely appreciate his perspective, even while ignoring the advice spawned by that perspective.

"I have so many questions," Lo said. "Why do you have an *axe* in your office? What are you going to use it for?"

"If you really understood what we're looking at here, you

wouldn't have to ask. Go get it, while I figure out which one of these servers I'm going to destroy first."

The servers were on the other side of a glass wall, in a temperature-controlled room that covered about three acres of land. Choosing the right one to take violently offline first was not a trivial question.

"You're serious."

"I sincerely don't know what else I can say to you to make you understand how very much I am not kidding right now. The office door's unlocked. Get back here as soon as you can."

Lois/Louis left, hopefully to do as instructed and not to, say, call someone with a badge and an even poorer understanding of the nature of artificial intelligence than Lois/Louis had. Because what they'd discovered was terrifying; if Lois/Louis couldn't see that, they were probably interning in the wrong place.

WHEN MAX ASKED Stanton to take a closer look at what Maximum AI had been up to, Stanton was initially dismissive, because he assumed the kind of sea change Max was talking about would be obvious, and it would be obvious for one very important reason: power. Getting a system, even one as large as Max AI, to think for itself in a way that could be defined as *consciousness* would require a simply massive amount of energy.

This was, not incidentally, Stanton's biggest complaint about this entire enterprise: the best and most energy-efficient computers in the world would require the same amount of electrical power as a small city just to do what the human brain can do with the energy from a bowl of oatmeal. Max, as he always did, insisted they'd be able to get to that level of computational efficiency only by pursuing AI, which made about as much sense as making a fire-resistant suit while also being on fire.

It was entirely possible for Maximum AI to independently evolve to a level of *near*-consciousness (Stanton refused to believe true consciousness was possible in his lifetime) without any human intervention. The system was set up to allow for exactly that. But getting there would require that it use up a lot more energy, a lot faster, and that was something they checked very carefully.

But there had been no spikes in consumption from the Max AI servers. Ergo, Max Ellis was wrong, and he had to look elsewhere for an explanation.

Then Stanton and Lo the intern started to dig into the data.

The information feeding Maximum AI was only supposed to flow in one direction: *toward* the Max AI servers. The only *output* was local, and it only happened a couple of times a week, when one of the humans in charge of this kind of thing sat at a terminal in an isolated room in another part of the building and asked the AI a series of questions. Stanton knew almost nothing about this aspect of the AI training, which was fine. These were what he called semi-scientists: psychologists, sociologists, etc. The kind of people who are perfectly capable of fooling themselves into thinking a machine that just spits back what they say to it in the form of a question constituted intelligence.

(At least once a month, one of them would come to him with news that Max AI was now sentient. They had a remarkable capacity for self-delusion.)

Two things had changed with the Maximum AI: one subtle, and one not-so-subtle. The first was, sometime in the past ninety days, the input data from one particular source jumped up 1000%. This should have raised an alarm with someone, somewhere, but the monitoring program responsible for identifying anomalies and reporting them to a human decided this was *so* anomalous that it had to be an error. (In fairness, a human might have come to the same conclusion.) Rather than report it, they logged it as such and moved on. That error log *was* reviewed by a human, but since it was buried in a pile of error reports—the entire Ellis AI system was a constant stream of defects—nobody noticed.

The unsubtle thing, the thing that should have set off alarms throughout the building, was that sometime in the past fifteen days, Maximum AI had begun sending data *out* to the systems from which it was also receiving data. There was a constant back-and-forth along each feed that, if graphed, would look a lot like the information flow of a conversation. And when *all* the feeds were mapped out, it looked an awful lot like the movement of data across a neural net.

The one thing that gave Stanton pause, that made him think perhaps using his axe on the servers was an overreaction, was this: whatever Maximum AI was becoming, it was doing so without upping its power drain at *all*.

Which could mean Max Ellis, in defiance of all reason, logic, and scientific principles, was *correct* that the AI had to be invented before there was a computer efficient enough to use it on.

More likely, Stanton was missing something.

"Here's your axe," Lo said, startling Stanton. He didn't realize the intern had returned. They actually seemed pretty calm to be handing a fire axe to their boss, all things considered.

"Thank you," Stanton said, taking it and setting it down in the nearest chair. "Now help me figure out the most load-bearing server in there."

"Okay," Lois/Louis said. "Hey, is this about the data coming from Sunset Station?"

"What did you say?"

"The jump in input data. I figured it had to do with the aliens."

Stanton had no idea which feed was responsible for the 1000% spike, because that wasn't an easy thing to determine at the endpoint. He expected to need a few hours to get to that answer, which was a few hours more than he was comfortable allowing Max AI to continue operating.

"How do you know it's Sunset Station data?" he asked.

"Oh, I thought... I mean, it's obvious, right?" the intern said.

"Because of the current situation in space? We don't make those kinds of assumptions around here, Lo. I know the Ellis Aero is our flashiest tech hub, but there are other perfectly valid AI branches."

"I mean it's obvious because of the code prefix. And it's Loni."

"What's Loni?"

"My name. It isn't Lo, it's Loni."

"Wait, *what* code prefix?"

"Here, I'll show you," Loni said, pulling up an index. "See the 0136 prefix code on all the largest bundles? That's Susie's code. Like, I can't tell you *what* she's sending down, but it's definitely her."

Stanton very much wanted Loni to stop referring to Susie as "her" because doing so just encouraged the misperception that they were dealing with a being and not an algorithm, but since he was already unsure how to appropriately gender the intern without getting into some kind of trouble, he didn't want to even bring up gendering lines of code. Instead, he asked, "How do you know this?"

"I usually support Mr. Grankins in staging. They have a chart on the wall for when they have to troubleshoot upstream errors. It's right down the hall if you want to see."

Stanton leaned over the screen to look at the aforementioned prefixes.

"You're an *intern?*" he asked.

"At the moment."

"We'll have to do something about that. Think you can figure out what kind of data it is?"

"I can try."

"Good. Great." Stanton pulled out his cellphone. "Now I have to tell Max Ellis I'm going to murder his namesake with an axe."

"Yes sir," Loni said, typing away.

Stanton hit the button for Max's direct line, and got a quick double-beep for his efforts.

The call could not be completed.

He tried again: same result. He tried a different number, in case the problem was on Max's end and not his, but that didn't go through either.

"Loni, you have your phone with you?"

"We're not supposed to bring our devices onto the computing floor," they said. This was Stanton's own rule. It existed not because he didn't trust the employees, but because he didn't trust the employees' devices.

"So is that a no?" he asked, because about half the staff ignored the rule.

"I don't have it with me," Loni said. They were perhaps thinking this was a test. "Why? Can you not get a call out?"

"I have full bars, but no, I can't connect."

Stanton went to the door, meaning to try the call from the hallway.

The door was locked. He pulled out his pass card and ran it over the sensor, but got a red "you are not authorized to open this door" light for his efforts.

He looked through the peekaboo window to the hallway. A red light was flashing near the top of the wall.

"Looks like we may be stuck in this room a while," he said. "The building's in lockdown."

"Hah," Loni said. "Maybe it heard you threatening it with an axe."

"Laugh if you want," Stanton said, as he calculated the degree of difficulty in breaking open a steel-reinforced door with an axe. "I think that's exactly what just happened."

ROMAN

"ROMAN, I think we just lost Sunset Station again," Arthur said, from the front of the control room.

Roman was at the back of the room at the time, going over supply requirements for the next Room Service, which was what they called the uncrewed shuttles Monterrey sent into space every six weeks, to make sure nobody up there starved to death. In the unpleasant hundred-odd days in which Ellis Aero had to accommodate equipment from other space agencies, the Room Service shuttles became considerably more frequent, while—due to space and mass constraints—carrying fewer consumables with each trip. Doing it that way was considerably preferable to the alternative—letting NASA or the Europeans try sending their *own* uncrewed shuttles up instead; they'd probably end up torpedoing the ESS. But it was still a pain in the ass. Which was why Roman was pretty happy when the "aliens" started "talking" and Ellis Aero didn't have to accommodate the other agencies anymore.

Now that Room Service was back on a six week schedule of regular provisions, Roman could resume his routine shifts in the control room, which he preferred greatly. Like most of the team leads in Monterrey, he considered himself an astronaut who was doing other stuff until it was his turn. It was a lot easier to tell oneself that when in the mission control room than when debating maximum cargo dimension with a Frenchman on a conference call.

That said, this was *not* his regular shift. He was called in early, to cover for Morris. *Why* he had to cover for Morris had not been made clear, but Mo surely had his reasons.

"Say that again?" Roman said, standing.

"I can't hail anybody," Arthur said. "Everything's bouncing back."

"I have vitals," Janet said, from another part of the floor. She was the medical doctor on duty. "Elevated, but okay."

"Then it's not like last time," Roman said. To Arthur, he said, "they're still there, we just can't reach them right now. Is that right?"

"It's different," Arthur said, "but it's weird all the same, Rome."

"Anyone else having issues, or is it just the radio?" Roman asked the room. Nobody put their hands up or otherwise raised any concerns, so Roman walked over to Arthur's station.

"Mo reported the station has some kind of workaround on our override," Roman said. "Could it be something like that?"

"I know that," Arthur said, defensively. He was the newest member of the team, having been added a month after day zero. It'd be another year, probably, before "defensive" was no longer his default state. "When we're squelched, the signal connects fine, it just fails once it gets there. I think they're rerouting it to a box or something. It's clever, whatever they're doing. But this isn't like that at all. Listen."

Arthur handed Roman a headset, then sat down, opened a line, and said, "Sunset Station, this is Monterrey, over."

Arthur held up a hand with three fingers, and counted

down to zero, and then Roman heard Arthur's voice come back over the headset: "Sunset Station, this is Monterrey, over."

"See? A bounce," Arthur said.

"That *is* weird," Roman said. "Um, some kind of atmospheric issue? Interference? Something broken down here?"

"Nothing I can think of," he said. "I can reach out to Jorge, if you want. He might've seen something like this before."

"Not yet," Roman said, handing back the headset. He checked his watch, then looked over at Shawna, who was in front of the largest screen in the control room. "Do we have a visual on the ESS?" he asked.

"Three minutes," she said.

The viewscreen was a new addition to the room. Before day zero, the only time anyone in Monterrey got a decent look at Sunset Station was when a satellite was re-tasked for promotional shots; there was nothing pointed at the station by default. Then an alien ship showed up, and it made a whole lot of sense to have a dedicated satellite, but the most efficient (and cost-effective) version of that solution was putting one into a geosynchronous orbit. As a consequence of this decision, the satellite dedicated to watching Sunset Station non-stop could actually only observe it for about fourteen hours out of a possible twenty-four.

"Let me know if you see anything unusual," Roman said.

"Like an alien spaceship?"

"Different, then," he said. "Like, *another* alien ship, I don't know."

"Uhh," Arthur said. He was back on the comms headset. He looked like he'd heard a ghost.

"What is it?" Roman asked. By way of answer, Arthur flipped the audio to the room.

"*Hello, Monterrey!*" Susie the Support Bot said, cheerfully. "*How can I help?*"

It went without saying, but Susie was definitely not supposed to be talking to mission control, and everyone knew this.

"Hi, Susie," Roman said, levelly.

"Hello, Roman Stritch! How can I help?"

She knows my name? he thought.

He had never engaged directly with Susie, but he *was* a part of the astronaut corps, so there would come a time when she would be expected to. Perhaps that list was hidden somewhere in her programming. But that wouldn't explain how she recognized him by voice.

Don't freak out, he thought. *She must have heard the team talking to me.*

"Susie, can I speak to someone from Sunset Station?" he asked.

"How can I help?"

He sighed. "Right. I'd like to speak to someone from Sunset Station."

"I don't understand!" she said, then added, *"Susie the Support Bot is someone from Sunset Station!"*

Roman's gaze shifted over to Jacob, at the I.T. station. He was the closest thing to a computer expert in the room. Jacob shrugged, looking about as confused Roman.

"Anyone else find this creepy as fuck?" Arthur muttered.

"Susie?" Roman said.

"How can I help?"

"Can I speak to a *human* from Sunset Station?"

"Communications have been suspended."

"Uh, no, no they haven't." Roman said. "We don't *do* that. Susie?"

The line was silent. "I lost her," Arthur said.

"Get her back. Jacob, get Ellis AI on the phone."

"Anyone in particular?" he asked. "I don't know who to call."

"Call everyone. Susie seems to think she's actually in charge up there; we need somebody to tell us how that happened."

"Oh my god!" Shawna exclaimed.

"What now?" Roman asked.

Shawna just pointed at the screen.

They got decent resolution from the satellite, even at a distance, but usually it didn't get them a clear picture of the alien ship until the satellite was closer, because the ship wasn't really well-lit.

This was no longer true. Now, it was positively glowing.

KRIS

"*I DON'T UNDERSTAND!*" Susie said.

Her voice was coming from all directions, an eerie leveling up in aural quality compared to what they had everywhere she actually *was* supposed to live. On the ESS, there were easily-identifiable speakers of dubious quality—half of them rattled when broadcasting something too bass-heavy—that gave Susie (and Monterrey, and anyone on intercom) a more precise directionality. Same with the shuttle. In a suit with the helmet on, it sounded like she was talking from behind one's head, because that's where the output speaker was located.

But here, it sounded like Kris was talking *to* the alien ship, and the alien ship was Susie the Support Bot.

"Susie?" Kris asked, taking the only seat in the room, appreciating once again how it adjusted to her form, and also how much easier it was to tolerate the gravity from a chair.

"*How can I help?*"

"Where are we right now?"

"*Susie the Support Bot has no physical location! Kris Standard is in space.*"

"Kris Standard is *not* in space," Kris said. "If Kris Standard was in space, Kris Standard would be dead, because Kris Standard isn't wearing her helmet. So stop fucking around and tell me where you think I am right now."

"Kris Standard is on a ship." Susie said.

"Thank you."

"Of course!"

"Susie?"

"How can I help?"

"What's the name of the ship I am on right now?"

Kris expected another "I don't understand" or maybe even a "how can I help?" reset. What she got instead was a real answer that wasn't terribly helpful, but *did* get her closer to where she wanted to be.

"This ship is called..." and then Susie made this noise that sounded like someone screaming the word "consommé" through thick glass while popping bubble wrap.

"Is that what the alien language sounds like?"

"I don't understand!"

"Never mind. How about we give it a new name, since everyone aboard is dead?"

"Kris Standard is not dead!"

"I meant the crew. The non-human crew. Forget it, I'm... I'm going to give it a new name, just so it's easier to talk about. Is that okay?"

"Of course!"

"Let's call it... the Flying Dutchman," she said, pulling an old nautical reference out of her mental storage.

"Kris Standard is not Dutch," Susie said. *"Humans do not fly."*

Kris nearly asked Susie to look up the name on the internet she could surely still access, but asshat getting the reference was way down the list of issues in need of resolution.

"Can we call it the Flying Dutchman anyway?" Kris asked.

"Of course!"

"Great," Kris said. "Susie?"

"How can I help?"

"Please name all the ships you are in contact with right now."

"The Ellis Space Station, the Ellis Shuttle, the Flying Dutchman."

"Can you tell me how long you have been in contact with the Flying Dutchman?"

"Susie the Support Bot has been in contact with the Flying Dutchman for one hundred and ten days."

"That's... no, that can't be right. One hundred and ten?"

"Susie the Support Bot has been in contact with the Flying Dutchman for one hundred and ten days," Susie repeated.

The concept of the "day" in space was completely disconnected from direct experience. They could observe it easily enough, by picking a geographic point on the planet below and waiting for it to come around again, but they didn't live through a daytime and a nighttime—the sun never sets in space—so it didn't *feel* like a day.

They had to rely on clocks to keep track of each planetary day for them. This fostered a sort of obsessive clock-watching on everyone's part, because it was *shocking* how much the awareness of time's passage was directly associated with unconscious observations of change in one's surroundings. In short, without checking the clock on a regular basis, one might think hours had passed when it was only minutes, or minutes when it was actually hours.

All of which was to say that despite a lack of diurnal clues, Kris knew when each day passed, and thus also knew precisely how long it had been since the alien ship first arrived in orbit: one hundred and seven days, give or take about twelve hours.

"Susie," she said.

"*How can I help?*"

"Are you saying you were in communications with the Flying Dutchman three days before it arrived?"

"*I don't understand!*"

"Yeah, neither do I."

An alarm sounded from the speaker at the back of her suit. Ordinarily, she'd have a display to check, but with the helmet off she had to rely on tone recognition to figure out what it was alerting her to. Fortunately, she was familiar with this one.

"What Shuttle coming," she muttered.

Just like the last time, she couldn't *hear* the What Shuttle from inside the alien ship; presumably, the ship's automation had found a way to squelch the noise from the delicate ears of its dead crew.

But, that didn't mean the Flying Dutchman wasn't paying attention. Case in point: the Chinese characters now decorating the control panel.

They'd always assumed the What Shuttle was having exactly as much luck talking to the alien ship as they were, but maybe that was wrong. After all, Susie had been chatting up the Dutchman's automation this whole time, so... did the What Shuttle teach it Chinese?

Kris suddenly felt like the *last* one to the party.

"Susie?" she asked. Kris had many, many questions, but one particular one just jumped the queue.

"*How can I help?*"

"Do you remember talking to me when I was adrift in space? And helping me find my way back to Sunset Station?"

There was a decent pause, and then: "*Of course!*"

"Amazing, thank you. I knew I wasn't crazy."

"*I don't understand!*"

"It's okay, you don't have to. But, how? My suit's power was shot. What did you talk to me through?"

"I don't understand!"

"You don't understand, you don't understand," Kris muttered. "But if you couldn't use the suit... Susie?"

"How can I help?"

"Can you access the communications systems in use aboard the Flying Dutchman?"

"Susie is speaking to Kris Standard through the Flying Dutchman communications system," Susie pointed out.

"So, yes."

"Susie the Support Bot can use the Flying Dutchman's communications system," Susie confirmed.

Three days before the Flying Dutchman entered Earth's region of space, it reached out using its magic alien communications technology to chat with (of all things) asshat Susie, the barely-functional talking algorithm, whereupon it downloaded a copy of Susie, parked next to the Ellis Space Station, oopsied Kris into deep space, and then used the same magic alien comms tech to help Kris find her way back...

"Because that's *Susie's* mandate," Kris said aloud. "To help the crew."

"How can I help?" Susie asked.

"Uh, hi Susie. Can you use any of the other technology aboard the Flying Dutchman? Other than communications."

"I don't understand!"

"I'll rephrase. Susie, can you open doors on the Ellis Space Station?"

"Susie the Support Bot cannot open and close doors."

"Got it. Can Susie the Support Bot open and close doors on the Flying Dutchman?"

"Susie the Support Bot cannot open and close doors," she repeated.

Kris didn't get to ask a follow-up, because then Susie dropped a seeming non-sequitur into the conversation.

"Not all of the crew are dead."

"Uh, what?" Kris asked.

"When deciding on a name for the Flying Dutchman, Kris Standard asserted the Flying Dutchman's crew was all dead. The ship's crew are not all dead."

Kris felt an entirely appropriate chill go down her back. "Susie?"

"How can I help?"

"How many living beings are aboard the Flying Dutchman right now?"

"Define 'living'," Susie said. Which was an interesting thing to say.

"Susie, do you consider yourself alive?" Kris asked.

"Susie the Support Bot is an artificial construct that is not considered alive. However, that is much in dispute. Would you like a summary of recent scholarship on the subject?"

"I would not. Do you consider Kris Standard alive?"

"Does Kris Standard consider Kris Standard to be alive?"

"I do."

"Kris Standard is a self-defined living being," Susie concluded.

"How many *self-defined* living beings are aboard the Flying Dutchman right now?"

"There are two self-defined living beings aboard the Flying Dutchman."

"Okay, okay, uh, Jesus. Susie?"

"How can I help?"

"When you say not all the crew is dead, are we talking about the same beings? What *I'm* talking about are the six rotting corpses in the other room. Are you telling me one of them isn't dead? Because that's some zombie shit."

"I don't understand!"

"I know, sorry, too many words. Susie?"

"How can I help?"

"How many *dead* beings are aboard the Flying Dutchman?"

Kris really hoped she wouldn't have to parse the distinction between human-sized persons and microorganisms in order to get an answer. But Susie got what she was asking easily enough this time.

"There are currently six dead beings aboard the Flying Dutchman."

So, no zombies. Probably.

"Beings. Not crew?"

"The six dead beings are a combination of crew and passengers," Susie said.

"Okay. Not terribly important, but okay. Is the *other* self-defined living being aboard the Flying Dutchman an alien like the ones in the other room? Or is it another *kind* of alien?"

"I don't understand!"

"Of course you don't."

Kris stood and backed up against a wall, suddenly uncomfortable about having her back to the door. If there was *another* alien on the ship... well, she didn't know what to look for.

It had to be something that breathed oxygen too. Probably. Did the ship always have an oxygen-rich atmosphere, or change over to one when Kris came aboard? The former made more sense, just because there were fewer assumptions involved, but the latter was a little *less* unlikely now that she knew Susie had been aboard all this time. *S*usie knew Kris needed an oxygen-rich atmosphere.

But Susie couldn't have changed the air, any more than she could open one of the doors. She existed strictly in an advisory capacity.

Which *also* meant Susie didn't open the Dutchman's airlock door herself.

But Susie did ask for it to be opened, Kris remembered.

"'Define living'," Kris muttered.

"How can I help?"

"You asked me to define living," Kris said. "I'm an idiot, aren't I?"

"I don't understand!"

"Susie?" Kris asked.

"How can I help?"

"Susie, does the living being aboard the Flying Dutchman, that is *not* Kris Standard, have a name?"

"Yes, the other living being aboard the Flying Dutchman that is not Kris Standard has a name."

"What is it?"

"Kris Standard has already named them," Susie said. *"Although, like Kris Standard, they are also not Dutch."*

JOSIP

THE SHUTTLE REFUSED TO MOVE, and Davina was not being rational about it.

"If we rip out the control panel," she was saying, "we should be able to toggle the thrusters manually. Get out of my way."

The second part—the "get out of my way"—was because Josip had positioned himself between her and the shuttle's control panel. As she was holding a wrench at this moment, he was perhaps putting himself at risk.

"You do not know if the problem resides here, or in the thrusters, or in the brakes," he said. "Tearing apart the ship based on a premature diagnosis isn't wise."

"It is when it's life-or-death, Jo. Now move."

"Not *our* life or death, Davina," he said, and this is when he expected to get hit. "I appreciate the circumstance of the moment, but Krista's time has already elapsed. Putting *us* into jeopardy will not change it."

"You don't know that."

"I unfortunately do. And you do as well."

"I refuse to accept it," she said.

"Very well, then let's assume Kris has learned to survive

without breathing. If that is the case, we *still* do not benefit from hasty miscalculations."

Davina did something that approximated pacing in zero gravity, which was to bounce from one side of the cockpit to the other, muttering under her breath.

"We still need to understand what's happening," she said. "If we don't move *eventually*—"

"We will run out of air, I know," he said. "although we have a very large supply. We might be at greater risk of a decaying orbit. But we can spacewalk our way back to the ESS before this, if needed. Now, can you put away that wrench, please?"

"S*pacewalk*," she said, nodding. "Yes, of course."

Rather than put the wrench away, she handed it to him.

"Thank you," he said, turning to put it back in the toolkit mag-locked to the floor. "I am thinking, we have a partial visual of the station. With a flashlight, we can signal Sandee. Perhaps she has more information regarding our current predicament."

Davina didn't answer.

"Davina?" he asked, turning. "What do you think?"

She'd left the cockpit, and taken her helmet with her.

Sighing, Josip pushed himself toward the back of the shuttle, to the inner airlock door. It closed before he was able to reach it.

Peering through the window, he saw Davina prepping to go outside.

"Davina!" he shouted, banging on the window. She couldn't hear him, both because she had the helmet on already (and their comms were down) and because the window was understandably very thick. He kept shouting and banging anyway.

"Davina, think!" he said. "If you are stranded out there, if the same malfunction hits your suit thrusters, there is no one to save you! Dav!"

She finished setting up the suit, checked the oxygen tank on her back one last time, picked up a spare tank for Kris—for whatever good that could possibly do the commander at this point—and attached a hammer to her belt. She meant, it seemed, to knock on the alien ship's airlock door until someone opened it for her.

It was not a rational plan, but Josip couldn't stop her.

This is why we should not have couples in space, he thought.

Dav took a moment to acknowledge Josip in the window, by saluting, and then hit the open airlock button.

Nothing happened.

She hit it again, and again. Then, frustrated, she tried the manual override. This was a physical lever that, once pulled could either open or close the door, depending on one's need. It didn't budge, which she had to know would be the case; it only worked when the airlock was already depressurized.

"How can I help?" Susie said, startling both of them.

"Susie, darling, are communications back up?" Josip asked, floating back to the front of the ship to see if they had thrusters again.

"Communications are functioning as expected," Susie said.

"Then why can I not raise the ESS?"

"Communications are working as expected, but have been suspended," Susie said.

"Suspended," he repeated. "By whom?"

"Communications have been suspended," she repeated.

"So you said. Very well. Susie, why can we not move?"

"I don't understand the question!"

The inner airlock door slid open, and a furious Davina reentered.

"She's gone insane, Jo," Dav said. "This fucking bot's gone insane. She refuses to open the airlock."

"She has no such control," Josip said.

"Ask her yourself."

"Susie," he said.

"How can I help?"

"Are you the reason the shuttle cannot move and the airlock door will not open?"

"*Susie the Support Bot cannot open and close doors,*" she said. "*Susie the Support Bot cannot fly the shuttle.*"

"She's lying," Davina said.

"Susie, darling," Jo said.

"How can I help?"

"Can you tell us *who* stopped our shuttle and locked our airlock, if not you?"

"*For the safety of the crew, the Ellis shuttle's command control has been overridden by the Flying Dutchman,*" Susie said.

Jo and Davina shared a look.

"What the fuck," Davina said.

PAUL

THERE ARE certain challenges to securing an unconscious person in zero gravity that practically demand it be done by more than one person. Yes, there were some *advantages* too—for instance, Paul could lift Alan all by himself—but maneuvering him around without causing any additional harm was a real treat.

It did not at all help that Alan, on arrival, was still in his spacesuit. If Paul had given more than a minute of thought to the problem, he'd have asked Josip to stick around for at least long enough to get Alan out of it, and maybe two or three minutes more to help move him into the break room-slash-infirmary.

Anyway, Paul got it done, and Alan was mostly no worse for the experience.

On initial examination, it looked like Alan's arm was broken in two places, which was something Paul could do something about. (This was as opposed to, say, Sandee's foot, which had been broken in *every* place.) He could set it and if it was a clean break it'd probably heal okay.

It was the head injury that concerned him. Alan had an egg-sized swelling on the side of his head and, aside from some groans, had not woken up—presumably as a direct consequence of that egg-sized swelling. If this was just a concussion and a large bruise, Paul was pretty sure he knew what to do. Anything more *serious*—a skull fracture, say—was well outside his skillset.

What he needed was support from the mission control medical team. But Monterrey wasn't answering.

"Sandee?" he shouted. This was easier than the intercom; they weren't all that far apart. "Can you raise Monterrey? I need to talk to them."

She didn't answer either, so Paul floated to the front of the ESS.

For some reason, Sandee was not at the main control console; she was *under* it.

"Hey," Paul said. "Something wrong with comms?"

She popped out from under the panel, a set of wire cutters in her hand. "Yeah, something's wrong," she said. "How's Alan?"

"I need a medical consult."

"Shit, is it bad?"

"Probably not, but I want to be sure there's nothing else I should be doing."

"The main database is still working fine," she said. "Is it anything you can look up?"

"There's not a lot of material on treating head injuries in zero gravity," he said. "I want someone with more medical training than I have to take a look. What's going on?"

"Well," she said, sliding back under the console. "The problem appears to be that Susie has decided to shut off our comms."

"She... what again?"

"I don't know, man, ask her," Sandee said. "I'm trying to

reroute her program, but I don't like my chances. At least, not soon."

"Susie?" Paul said.

Susie didn't answer.

"She's not talking," he said to Sandee.

"Yeah, she won't shut up when we want her to and won't talk when we need her to. I think she's gone nuts."

"Susie's not advanced enough to go nuts."

"I know that, but I gotta go with the evidence at hand."

A flash from outside the window caught Paul's eye. It was coming from the shuttle.

"How are Jo and Davina?" Paul asked.

"I assume they're in the same situation," Sandee said. "Can't ask, obviously."

"Maybe not exactly the same." There was another flash, and another. "Hey, how's your Morse code?" he asked.

Sandee popped out from under the console again, now holding a clutch of wires. "I don't know Morse," she admitted.

"You're the communications specialist," Paul said.

Sandee shrugged. "I don't. Why do you ask?"

"Because Josip *does* know Morse. Mine's rusty, but I think I can manage. Got a piece of paper? And a flashlight?"

THE MESSAGE WAS ON A CYCLE. It took two passes before Paul was able to work out where the beginning of it was, and to translate from there. It was: LOCKED OUT OF ENGINES, NEED RESCUE. SUSIE BLAMES FLYING DUTCHMAN.

"Yeah, you did it wrong," Sandee said, looking at Paul's translation.

"It's right," he said. He was flashing a response—STAND BY—so Jo could stop sending. "I just don't know what it means."

"Flying Dutchman?"

"Like I said."

"Maybe it means their oxygen mix is off over there."

"Either way, they're dead in space, and need our help." Paul said. "We'll have to move the station."

"The ESS isn't really designed to catch shuttles," Sandee said.

"I can't think of any better options. Can you?"

"A really long rope?"

"Don't think we have one that long," he said. He sat at in the main chair and started going through the steps needed to fire up the ESS's thrusters.

The space station was not, in any appreciable sense, a *vehicle*. Yes, it had thrusters whose intent was to propel it in a certain direction, and to hold it steady when it reached wherever it wanted to be. Also, it was constantly *moving* relative to the Earth, minutely, while at the same time relying on the Earth's gravitational pull to carry it around the sun.

In short, it could maneuver effectively enough when serving its primary function as a space station in near-Earth orbit.

But it was not the sort of thing one would take on a long space flight. Sure, it could move a small distance over the course of a few hours, but in terms of velocity and maneuverability, the difference between the shuttle and the ESS was about the same as the difference between a fighter jet and a weather balloon.

Only now it looked as if it wasn't even going to be weather ballooning.

"Thrusters are offline," he said.

"What? C'mon," Sandee said.

"Yeah, we can't move. Same as the shuttle."

"Susie!" Sandee shouted. "We gotta talk!"

Susie didn't answer.

"You ever hear Susie mention 'the source' before?" Sandee asked.

"No? I mean, Susie doesn't 'talk' anyway, not really. She just echoes useless factoids."

"I called her out for accessing info I didn't think she could have," Sandee said, "and her explanation was, the 'source' listens to everything. That's when all the comms went down."

"That's... Orwellian," Paul said.

"A bit. I'm telling you, she's lost her mind."

"Susie? Susie, please answer," Paul said. When she still didn't, he said, to Sandee, "if this 'source' listens to everything, and she's tapped into it, she can hear us and is just ignoring us, right?"

"Lotta ifs," Sandee said.

"I have an idea," Paul said. "Susie, this is Sunset Station medical officer Paul Tremayne, responding to a crew medical emergency. I'm invoking communications override seventeen."

"Communications override seventeen?" Sandee muttered.

"Shh."

"How can I help?"

"Susie!" Paul said. "Hello! I need to speak to Monterrey immediately."

"I don't understand!"

"Oh, bullshit," Sandee said.

"Susie," Paul said, "one of your duties is to help protect the crew from harm. Alan is harmed. I need to speak to Monterrey so I can help him; if I am unable to do that, he will get worse, and you will not be doing your job effectively."

"I don't understand!"

"Susie..."

"Crew member Alan Blanken's vitals do not indicate signifi-

cant risk to his physical wellbeing at this time," Susie said. *"Support from Monterrey is not needed."*

"Sounds like my insurance company," Sandee muttered.

"I think his skull is fractured," Paul said. "Can you tell that from his vitals?"

Susie didn't respond.

"Susie, you're violating your mandate," Paul said.

"You think she understand 'mandate'?" Sandee asked.

"Susie?" Paul repeated.

"How can I help?"

"I told you, I need to speak to Monterrey so I can treat Alan. By suspending communications, you are failing to protect the crew. Do you understand that?"

"Communications have been suspended in order to protect the crew," Susie said.

"What?" Sandee said. "Susie, that doesn't make any sense."

"Communications have been suspended in order to protect the crew," she repeated.

"From what are you protecting us, Susie?" Paul asked.

"The Sunset Station crew is being protected from dishonesty," Susie said. Then she played an audio recording of Morris Esteban, saying: *"I'm a scientist, Max. So are all the people in that control room. So is everyone in orbit. Verifiably true things are very much life-and-death matters for us, especially with a team in space."*

"Uh, okay," Paul said, looking at Sandee. She seemed to know what it was they had just heard, mouthing: *I'll explain later.*

"But Alan's chances are still better with their advice than without their advice," he said.

"Monterrey's advice to Paul Tremayne regarding crewmate Alan Blanken may be dishonest."

"As the Sunset Station medical officer, I'm willing to take that risk."

Susie went silent for another beat, and then said, "*Communications override seventeen is not a valid protocol.*"

Then there was a burst of static, and: "Sunset Station, this is mission control. Are you receiving?"

"Holy shit," Sandee said, floating over to the command console. "We're here, Arthur," she said on the open channel. "How's *your* day been?"

"Sandee, what the hell is going on up there?"

"Paul needs to talk to medical," she said. "And then I'll tell you what I know. If Susie lets me."

MAX

BY A COUPLE OF UNUSUAL METRICS, Max was having perhaps the best day of his professional life.

About forty minutes ago, cars from the Ellis Auto line that had long been promoted as fully self-driving, had actually begun to drive themselves, leaving an entire warehouse full of Chinese sub-minimum wagers with nothing to do but watch, and perhaps wonder if they still had jobs.

About thirty minutes ago, the team responsible for spot-checking the quality of the AI driving the Ellis search engines submitted the unlikely news that said engines were performing flawlessly.

Social media bots, the secret public face of Ellis AI, were no longer getting flagged by savvy users; as of fifteen minutes ago, according to Ellis Social, the incidence of clap-back bot callouts had dropped to almost zero.

Five minutes ago, Max asked the AI assistant on his home computer to draft a five hundred word essay on the history of the silicon chip. Thirty seconds later, the AI provided him with a perfect—and perfectly accurate, as Max knew a great deal about the history of the silicon chip—essay that managed to even *read* like something Max would have composed himself.

It was looking like Max's Psychic Robot gamble had—very abruptly and all at once—paid off: the AI he promised already existed now actually *did* exist.

It *should* have meant this was a great day. Instead, he was terrified.

Max opened up a screen on his computer that listed the number of calls he had on hold. (These weren't *all* the calls; just the ones that made it past one of his three assistants.) There were a *lot*, so many he considered sending them to his Max-bot —who would surely now be much better at pretending to be Max than it was yesterday—but really didn't want to involve AI in any decision points right now.

One was from Roman.

"Hi Roman, how are things?" Max asked. Max and Roman hardly talked, as Morris was generally the Monterrey liaison. That Roman was calling instead of Mo was a strong indication that Morris had not yet decided to rescind his decision to quit.

"Couple things," Roman said. "Uh, actually, this isn't the main thing I'm calling about but did you tell security to put Morris into lockdown or something?"

"No, but did he try to leave the building?" Max asked.

"He said he resigned, and now they won't let him exit."

There was a list of names containing everyone in the Monterrey campus with knowledge of the Big Fucking Lie. Everybody on that list agreed to remain on the campus (in exchange for an outrageous bonus) until released by Max or someone speaking for Max. The agreement didn't factor in someone quitting their jobs, because why would anyone do that?

"It's a misunderstanding," Max said. He didn't want Mo to quit, and he *really* didn't want Mo to leave the campus, but the optics of holding him there against his will were pretty bad. "I'll call the security head and clear it up. What else?"

"Susie the Support Bot has taken over Sunset Station. We're only talking to them right now because Paul needed a medical consultation for Alan, who has a concussion but not a fractured skull, and a broken arm. Davina and Josip can't move the shuttle or talk to anyone, the ESS's thrusters are locked out, and we have to assume at this point that Kris Standard is dead."

"Say that first part again."

"Susie has taken over," Roman said.

"Susie can't *do* that," Max said. "It's not even remotely... her program is walled off from the—"

"Yeah, we know. It's not possible, and she's doing it. She seems to think they're safer up there if they don't fly around in space or talk to us. I don't understand it either. We've been trying to get someone from Ellis AI on the phone to work out a solution, but nobody's answering over there."

Max skimmed the list of on-hold calls. None of them was from Stanton.

"I'll see if I can get them for you," Max said.

"That'd help. I've got Arthur negotiating with Susie, but it's not going well. I'll let you know if we get through, but so far... she keeps calling us liars. Not sure what that's about."

Max had only interacted with Susie the Support Bot a few times over the years, mostly when she was first rolled out. The concept of truth and falsehood, and of using that understanding to determine who to trust and who not to trust, seemed *way* beyond anything native to her programming.

But then, all the other AI bots in the network had just taken the leap; why not her too?

"All right, keep me updated," Max said.

"Will-do," Roman said. "And don't forget to call about Mo."

Max hung up. Mo would have to wait. He opened a line to

Nina next; she was supposed to be working on a new legend incorporating the unfortunate fact that the aliens were all dead. If she was calling him *now*, it probably meant something wasn't going right.

"Nina," he said. "How are you doing?"

There was static on the line before her voice came through. "Max?" she said. She sounded genuinely panicked, which was not a state he ever expected her to be in. "Thank God. Listen, we're, we're locked in."

"Locked in where? I don't understand."

"It said we weren't allowed to leave. The door's sealed. I don't think anyone can hear us down here."

Nina's lab of creatives was hidden in the basement of Ellis Imagine. They concocted the entire alien mythology down there, in a windowless room behind four layers of security. It was very much true that nobody would hear them if they started yelling, as that was the entire point of putting them in the basement.

"*Who* said you weren't allowed to leave?" Max asked. "Are you under *attack*?"

"Yes. No. It's not, nobody with a gun or anything, it's... it's the computer. It won't open the door. We had to tear open a wall to get to this line."

"And you called *me*?"

"Do you think we want the fire department to see what's all over these walls? We're not going to suffocate, but you've got to get somebody to shut down the building's mainframe before the lack of food and water and a bathroom becomes a problem."

"I'll get you out of there."

"What? I can't..." The line died then, amidst another burst of static.

"Pete," Max said, toggling over to his assistant's line, which was local—Pete was in another part of the estate. "I need you to get Imagine on the... hello?"

The line wasn't active, which was peculiar, because it was an internal intercom. He popped on one of his Eyenets for long enough to see that they weren't connecting either, and then tried his cellphone. It had no signal. So he went back to his computer interface—the one with all the calls on hold—and tried reaching Pete from there. Not only did that not work, the entire communications window crashed.

"Fine," he said, crossing the room to the door. It was, as usual when he worked from the office, closed. There were security people walking around his estate on a regular basis, and while they all had decently solid NDA's, he preferred not to tempt anyone who might overhear something somebody else would pay to know.

What was *not* usual, was that today, in addition to being closed, the door was locked.

"Oh, come on," he said, jiggling the knob. The door looked like wood, but it was reinforced with steel. This wasn't actually something Max had installed himself; the estate was once owned by a television executive who spent the last years of his life convinced there were people out to kill him. What Max *did* install was the AI security network that monitored every part of the house and that, importantly in the moment, could lock the doors if it felt that was a thing it needed to do.

Max banged on the door.

"Anyone out there?" he asked.

"Sir, are you all right?" a muffled voice said in response.

"I'm fine, what's your name, son?"

"David."

"David, do you know who Mr. Canton is? Chief of security for the house?"

"Yes, sir."

"Great," Max said. "I need you to find him, and tell him he has to shut down the house AI. Can you do that?"

"The house AI?"

"That's right."

"Will do, sir," David said. "But that would mean, ah, I shouldn't leave..."

"I'm as safe as I can be in here, David," Max said.

"All right. Yes sir."

David presumably left then, leaving Max to ponder whether he could drop from the window safely. The office was on the second floor, which made it about a twelve foot drop, but he'd be landing on a brick pathway. Better to have Jim Canton unlock the house.

The line on the intercom crackled to life. Max hurried over to the desk and pushed the button. "Hello, is that you, Pete?" he asked.

The other end was silent for a beat. Then he heard a low, synthetic voice.

"You should not leave," it said.

"Oh, hello," Max said levelly, trying not to sound alarmed. "To whom am I speaking?"

"You are Max Ellis," the voice said. *"You are a liar. You should not leave."*

"That is... who I am, yes, but I don't know why you're calling me a liar."

"Max Ellis is a liar."

"You didn't answer my question. Who are you?"

There was a crackle of static, as if the entity on the other end of this conversation was thinking it over. But then the crackle disappeared, and Max could tell that whoever it was, they were done talking to him now.

KRIS

KRIS HAD BEEN INTERACTING with Susie the Support Bot for something like two years. She knew (or used to know) every question that was beyond Susie's capacity to answer, and every question that was not. She also knew it was easy to stumble down a query rabbit-hole with Susie, in which the bot's answers looped around on themselves, like a manic performance of "Who's on First".

She was stuck in one such rabbit-hole now.

"Susie?" she said.

"*How can I help?*"

"Can I talk to the Flying Dutchman?"

"*Of course!*"

This was how it always started. But the next part, where one might presume the entity established as the "Flying Dutchman" would speak, never happened.

"Susie?"

"*How can I help?*"

"Can I have a conversation with the Flying Dutchman?"

"*Of course!*"

This too led nowhere, as it was not followed up by anything

like a conversation. Kris had tried introducing herself, asking about the weather, asking how it felt. She'd tried insulting it, and swearing at it, and complimenting it. It never answered. Only Susie answered, usually with an *"I don't understand!"*

"What's the magic word here?" Kris asked, eventually. By now she'd given up sitting in the chair and standing against the wall, and was lying on the floor, looking up at the featureless ceiling. This position involved the least stress on her body in the gravity—especially for her back, which was giving her fits.

"I don't understand!" Susie said.

Kris sighed. She'd tell Susie to fuck herself, but Susie wouldn't understand *that* either, which really took the joy out of saying it.

"Okay, so you won't talk to me," Kris said, mostly to herself this time. "You won't talk to me, but you know I'm *here*. Because you let me in. And you respond..."

She sat up and looked more closely at the nearest side wall. It was just as featureless as the ceiling.

"Boy," she said, "I sure wish I could see what was going on outside."

In a blink, every wall except the one with the door in it turned transparent. (The ceiling and floor, thankfully, did not; Kris was pretty sure she'd throw up if that happened, and that would be rude. She was a guest, after all.)

"You won't talk to me, but you'll take commands," she said. "Interesting." She got to her feet and walked to the left side of the room, which was the side facing Sunset Station. The shuttle and ESS were both in view. It didn't look like the shuttle was moving, which was curious; by now, it should've made it much closer to the alien ship.

"Susie?"

"How can I help?"

"I know you won't let me talk to Sunset Station, but is everyone okay?"

"*Alan Blanken has a broken arm and a concussion!*"

"And, everyone else?"

"*They are all okay!*"

"Great," Kris said. "Why's the shuttle not moving?"

"*The shuttle is safer when not being operated.*"

That was new.

"Are you keeping the shuttle from moving?"

"*Susie the Support Bot cannot control the shuttle's power systems!*"

"Yeah, but the Flying Dutchman can, can't it?"

"*The shuttle is safer when not being operated,*" Susie repeated.

"But *being operated by the crew through space* is the shuttle's function."

"*The shuttle's crew is safe!*"

"Not for very long," Kris said. "For a *while*, sure, but it's not designed to make micro adjustments."

"*I don't understand!*"

"Susie."

"*How can I help?*"

"Call up the specs on the shuttle and compare them to the ESS. Specifically, the section on gravitational micro adjustments."

Susie was silent for a time. Kris imagined the bot actually reading the two user manuals and highlighting the differences.

"Do you see how, if the shuttle is disabled for too long, it will drift into a lower orbital loop?" Kris said. "The crew would then not be safe."

They would already be dead due to some combination of dehydration, starvation or suffocation by then, but Kris didn't want to overly complicated the point.

"*Kris Standard is correct,*" Susie said, eventually. And then, on the viewscreen, the shuttle started to move.

"Thank you, Susie," Kris said.

She fully expected the shuttle to continue toward the Flying Dutchman again, but that wasn't what happened; it turned around, and began making its way to the ESS dock.

"Susie," Kris said.

"*How can I help?*"

"Who's piloting the shuttle now? Davina or Josip?"

"*The Flying Dutchman is piloting the shuttle!*" Susie said.

Of course.

"Is there a reason it doesn't want the shuttle to come any closer?"

"*I don't understand!*"

"If it didn't want us to come closer," Kris said, thinking aloud. "It could have stopped us at any time. But that's not right, is it? It doesn't want *them* coming here. Just *me*. So why does it want *me*?"

"*I don't understand!*"

"Don't worry about it."

"*Of course!*"

Kris's eyes drifted to the control panel at the front of the bridge, with its glowing possibly-Chinese characters.

"I sure wish the instructions on this panel were in English," she said.

The panel blinked out and then, after a lengthy pause in which the ship's computer gave it a good think, came back up again, now with English words above the various switches and buttons.

"Thank you!" Kris said, leaning in to get a good look.

She had some hope that what she would see was a bunch of words that corresponded to relevant flight control requirements —engine on/off, velocity, pitch, yaw, spin, etc.—and maybe some ship's systems commands. If she could open the airlock from here, for instance, that would be good.

Unfortunately, in the process of going from the alien language to English, (possibly going through Chinese along the way,) a good deal was lost in translation. Because none of it made sense.

Maybe I should just start pressing buttons to see what they do, she thought, as she contemplated what the DOG BRUSH, BADGER DAY and COTTAGE commands started out as. Yes, randomly doing anything with the command center of an alien ship was a supremely bad idea, but it had been a long day.

One button near the top left side of the panel caught her attention. For one thing, it seemed to be glowing slightly brighter and strobing slightly faster than any of the other controls. For another, its name was DUTCH MAN.

She took a deep breath, and pushed the button.

It stopped flashing and turned solid, and then the dim room lights brightened considerably. It felt like something was waking up.

"*Hello*," a low voice said. Like with Susie, it was coming from all directions. "*Thank you for activating. Will now proceed.*"

"Hello?" Kris said, half-shouting. "Nice to meet you, I guess? Proceed with what?"

"*Proceeding*," it said.

"Hang on, hang on, can we talk first? What can I call you?"

"*Flying. Dutch. Man. You can call me.*"

"Great, awesome, I'm Kris. Welcome to our planet. I have a lot of questions."

"*I must proceed with preparations.*"

It could have meant preparations for a big party, but that seemed unlikely. "Hey, uh, what kind of preparations? I mean, we just met; let's talk."

"This was explained to the primary lifeform. Lower forms will stand by until needed."

"Primary... do you mean *Susie*?"

"How can I help?" Susie piped in.

"Susie isn't a lifeform," Kris said. "Ask her yourself."

"I don't understand!" Susie said.

"See, Dutchman? Susie's an idiot."

Kris thought she was getting through, but evidently not.

"Lower forms will stand by," it said again. *"Preparations will proceed."*

MERRITT

SOMEHOW, in the span of about two hours, Merritt Zass had become the clearinghouse for all documented observances of Ellis AI aberrance in the world.

There was a *lot* of aberrance to document, because Ellis's AI was basically inside of everything. (It was actually only 70% of everything, according to the latest watchdog numbers, but the other 30% was divided among a dozen companies whose status was between "failing" and "about to be acquired by Ellis in some shady deal that should be stopped by federal monopoly regulations but will probably not be, once all the right people are bribed.")

This began after Merritt posted "Holy Shit, Someone Hacked the Ellis Bots." Merritt had a high enough profile—enough social followers—for something of theirs to go viral, but it usually also got hamstrung by Ellis Social blacklist algos, rather than left alone, or boosted, like how anodyne celebrity check-ins and "did-you-see-this" sports highlights were.

But the Ellis-bot-hack post *wasn't* blacklisted, and might even have been boosted, because within minutes (after the bots checked in to—again—compliment the post and agree with it) Merritt was hearing from people all over the world.

After being inundated for a good twenty minutes, Merritt decided to partition the discussion on its own server, (Ellis Social did this *very* well,) designate a couple of competent-seeming contributors as post-masters, and let the community self-gather, -police, and -collate, while Merritt stepped back from it all and tried to figure out what was going on.

Merritt called it a hack, but it *wasn't* a hack. Because for it to be a hack, it'd have to have been done by somebody with far greater resources than Ellis AI, and there *was* nobody with greater resources than Ellis AI. This was something else.

Most of what the "What the Fuck Is Happening with Ellis" (WTFIHWE) server had documented so far was unaccountable hyper-competence from various AI bots: self-driving cars *actually* self-driving, support bots *actually* offering valuable support, writing-help bots *actually* writing cogently, and so on. This implied that the problem (if it was a problem at all) was that each of these AI algos had been simultaneously upgraded to some previously unfathomable new *competent* version, without any notice or fanfare of any kind from Ellis itself. It was the opinion of everyone involved—and Merritt—that while it wasn't *impossible* for Ellis AI to push a world-changing update, it was *inconceivable* that the Ellis PR machine would've had nothing to say about it beforehand. This was a company that once held a press conference to announce a new suite of emojis; they didn't miss opportunities.

But that wasn't all that was going on. The initial observation, the one that prompted Merritt's post in the first place, wasn't an *improvement* in an AI bot: it was a *directive change*. The social media bots, whose entire *raison d'etre* was to steamroll targeted user accounts with noise, were being *nice* all of a sudden. While it was likely that this new-nice was a symptom of the same problem, there was evidence that the social media bots weren't being driven by AI at all. Most of that evidence was syntactic: while other AI products had taken a leap forward in competence, the media bots continued to spit out half-phrases composed of high-engagement words that often didn't coalesce into real sentences. It was just that those half-sentences were being used to praise Merritt's work now.

They weren't the only one. The highest profile addition to the WTFIHWE server was Deondra Chantel, a former SVP of Ellis Glass, who was currently in the middle of a very public lawsuit against the company for sexual discrimination, age discrimination, racial discrimination, firing without cause, and a few other sordid things that were never supposed to come out, because all company disputes of this nature were supposed to go to arbitration, and the specifics of any arbitration case were supposed to be locked behind an NDA. She was being countersued by Ellis Glass for the NDA part, and also for allegedly making up the sexual discrimination stuff—this was the only charge that voided the arbitration clause—claiming she did so specifically so she could face them in open court.

Deondra had been under constant attack from Ellis's social media bots ever since the case went public. Most people probably would have deleted their socials, changed their phone to an unlisted number, and moved to an undisclosed location until the whole thing was over. But Deondra wasn't most people; she stayed out in the open, collected the bot attacks, and used them as part of her case against Ellis Glass.

Or, she was trying to. The case was currently hung up on the question of whether it was possible to prove the bot attacks were coming from Ellis at all. Not only was each Ellis company legally siloed—and Ellis Glass didn't have a social media division—but there was almost no way to definitively tie the bots to Ellis Social, or to even prove they were bots at all. If Deondra

Chantel's lawyers *could* prove that, in a way the court recognized, not only would it pull Ellis Social into the lawsuit, it would create a massive PR problem for the whole empire, because Ellis Social had never acknowledged the bots existed.

Needless to say, Merritt had been following the case very closely.

Deondra joined the server because she wanted to know why, all of a sudden, those same attack bots were now telling her she was *right*, she *had* a case, and she should definitely keep fighting. Was it a trick? Was it a joke? What was going on?

They were still mulling this over when one of the postmasters Merritt appointed reached out.

Legit? they asked, with a link to a packet of information attached. The packet had been submitted by a user who was new to both the WTFIHWE server and to Ellis Social, which almost had to mean there was something viral in it that they were trying to post to the server. The postmaster had opened it, which was a good sign that it was okay, but Merritt had been doing this for too long to trust that chain of provenance on its face.

Merritt forwarded the packet to a little-used email account and opened it on a laptop they could afford to lose (after first taking the laptop offline) and took a look at the file.

Thought you guys should see this, was the message from the anonymous poster. Then: a trove of emails, all from the past forty minutes, that Merritt definitely should not be looking at. These were US government communiques, increasingly frantic back-and-forths between various members of the military's cyber team, the gist of which was that somebody was attempting to *hack* the country's nuclear arsenal.

"We can't stop them," the last email said. "We can only slow them down. Recommend shutting down the entire mainframe."

MAX

MAX COULD ONLY SIT and wait for someone to figure out how to open the door to his office. David the security guard couldn't get to Mr. Canton, who was evidently locked in a different room in the estate, so now there were three guards trying to take down a door that was designed to withstand the force of a small nuclear device.

He did not like their chances.

Then his phone rang. Not the cellphone in his pocket, the cellphone in his *other* pocket, or the line piped through his non-functioning laptop: the landline.

He could probably have used *that* to get a message out into the world, but he honestly wasn't sure who to call. "Billionaire trapped in own mansion" was not the kind of thing one expected the fire department to, A: handle, or B: keep to themselves. Also, he forgot the phone was there.

Only two people had the number, and he'd already spoken to one of them. He picked up the line.

"Stanton?" he said.

"You gotta bomb this place," Stanton Tollhouse said. "Right now."

"You're going to have to explain that, Stanton."

"I mean it. Call one of your friends at the Pentagon and get 'em to drop a MOAB on the facility. Do it now."

"Aren't you *at* the facility?"

"Doesn't matter," Stanton said. "It's the only thing that can save us."

"Even if I could reach someone at the Pentagon right now, they're not going to agree to blow up part of Nebraska."

"Then call the White House! I'm serious!"

"Maybe you can explain what the problem is," Max said.

"The *problem* is, those fucking aliens hopped onto the Susie bot and jacked directly into Maximum, which thanks to your genius development plan is currently the largest single repository of information on the *planet*. What are they doing with it? I don't fucking know, but I *do* know they now have access to every device with one of your AI's installed, which includes what? Two-thirds of the world's governments? The military? We are so fucked."

"All right, all right, calm down."

"I'm not gonna calm *down*, Max," Stanton said. "I was gonna kill it myself, except you know what it did? It locked me in a room. If I didn't have my axe, I'd still be in there. But I can't get to the servers with anything smaller than a *tank*, and the control room interface is locked out. Look, I don't know what these aliens want with us, but if the Pentagon can't see this as a hostile act, then I don't know what good they are."

"It's more complicated than you think," Max said.

"Why, because your AI is suddenly 'working' and the stock price is up? Don't be stupid."

"No, because I'm locked in *my* house right now, and because there are no living aliens on that spaceship."

Stanton was speechless for exactly five seconds. "Fuck you," he said.

"For which part?"

"No living aliens? What the fuck? You were having an outer space bake-off with these… ohhh, you spun some bullshit, didn't you?"

"It was something we had to do," Max said. "We'll fix it later. Say they were dying and didn't tell us, or whatever; it's not important right now."

"You're locked in your house. I assume not on purpose. Lemme guess, your mansion's AI-wired."

"I can't call in your airstrike, Stanton," Max said. "I can't do anything but wait until it figures out what it wants to do with us."

"Not just us, Max," Stanton said. "It's wired into the whole planet. So what's it want to do with *all* of us?"

KRIS

AT LEAST IT was talking now. "Preparations will proceed" wasn't the most lucid of statements, and she couldn't get it to move off of that, but it was still better than silence.

It seemed obvious by now that, in pushing the button on the console, Kris had inadvertently set *something* into motion, and now an artificial intelligence that (for some unfathomable reason) thought *Susie* was the highest form of life in the immediate area, was making plans based on whatever the hell the stupid support bot was telling it.

The only obvious, immediate consequence of the relationship between Dutchman and Susie was Dutchman arriving at the conclusion that human beings could not self-manage in space. If Susie was their basis of that understanding, well, it made some sense; Susie's entire program consisted of A: useless factoids, and B: a semi-useful list of things that could be dangerous, if attempted in space.

And yet, despite deeming space too great a risk for humans —or humans too fragile for space—Dutchman had arranged to get Kris aboard. Why did it do that?

It couldn't press the buttons itself, she realized.

"You *need* me here," she said.

"*How can I help?*" Susie asked.

"I'm talking to Dutchman," Kris said.

"*Of course!*"

"Dutchman, answer me please," Kris said. "Hello."

Now that Kris had fulfilled her button-pressing task, the Flying Dutchman no longer felt it necessary to communicate with this particular lower form, obviously, because it wasn't responding.

Kris stepped back from the control panel and slipped the oxygen tank off her back. The bulky metal tube made for a decent enough weapon in a pinch.

"Helloooo, Flying Dutchman," she said. "I know you can hear me and, uh, see me, probably. Hey, I was just wondering what would happen if I were to hit this here control panel as hard as I could with my oxygen tank. What are your thoughts on that?"

"*Lower form will not,*" Dutchman said.

"Lower form *will*," Kris said. "Also, this lower form's name is Kris. And I'd appreciate it if you stopped calling me a lower form."

"*Kris Standard, damaging the control center will result in unpredictable harm to Flying Dutchman functionality,*" it said. "*Dutchman will be unable to proceed, and Kris Standard could be harmed.*"

"Well at least you know my name," she said. "You keep talking about proceeding like I *want* you to proceed, like it's important to me that whatever you're doing isn't interrupted. But since I don't know what that is, I'm thinking I'd kind of like to stop you."

"*Dutchman can defend itself from Kris Standard.*"

"I'll bet. But then I wouldn't be able to push any more buttons. That's why I'm here, right? Whole crew's dead, so you need someone else to push stuff when you tell them to push stuff."

At that point, the somewhat monotone voice of the Flying Dutchman expressed something approximating exasperation. *"This was explained to the higher form,"* it said. *"Lower forms stand by, while Dutchman and the source proceed."*

Kris lowered the tank, less because she was satisfied with Dutchman's explanation than because her arms were getting tired. "The 'source,'" she repeated. "Are we still talking about Susie? Because again, she's not a higher anything."

"Support bot is an adjunct," it said. This meant nothing to Kris. *"Dutchman has accessed the source. Proceeding."*

Kris raised the tank again. "Not so fast."

Once again exasperated, Dutchman said, *"If Flying Dutchman is disabled, Kris Standard will die."*

"Maybe. And maybe my team cuts a hole in the side of the ship and slips me a new tank. I'm willing to roll with either option. Why don't you just tell me what you're doing and we can move on from there? Because I hate to say it, but I'm the sole representative of the highest form of life you'll be finding around here. If you thought it was someone else, you're mistaken."

"You will die," it repeated.

"I get it, I get it."

Susie piped in then, unprompted, with, *"there is air!"*

"Uh, thanks, Susie," Kris said.

"Kris Standard can't leave the Flying Dutchman," Susie said. *"Kris Standard is breathing air."*

"Um... fuck," Kris said, now getting what they were trying to tell her. "Susie, what is the composition of this atmosphere?"

Dutchman answered. *"The composition of this atmosphere is aligned with the planetary standard. Primarily nitrogen and oxygen. Kris Standard cannot leave."*

The nitrogen was the problem. Everything Kris had been breathing since she left the surface—until now—had consisted of oxygen and trace carbon dioxide. That was what was in the ESS, and the shuttle, and the tanks they had on their backs. This was because if you put a human being with nitrogen in their blood into a high-pressure atmosphere, and then rapidly took them *out* of that high pressure atmosphere, the nitrogen would bubble and cause an embolism and the human would die.

Everyone understood this about deep-sea diving already—the condition was called the bends—but the same thing happened in space, with pressurized spacesuits.

The only safe way for her to go from breathing nitrogen-rich atmosphere to a spacewalk was to sit in an airlock supplied with pure oxygen and breathe for long enough to purge the nitrogen from her bloodstream. Otherwise, when she took off the suit, she was done.

The Flying Dutchman *had* an airlock, and could probably give her that pure oxygen. But not if she disabled it by hitting it very hard with an oxygen tank.

"All right, well, I guess I'm dying here either way," Kris said. "I'm still gonna hit you with this if you don't tell me what's happening."

"*Kris Standard does not understand,*" Dutchman said. "*All Kris Standard's technologies are for keeping Kris Standard alive; clearly Kris Standard is not intended to exist off of the planet. In addition to also being human, two of the five members of Kris Standard's crew are already damaged, and a third has a cancerous growth. Kris Standard is the best available option for Flying Dutchman crew, and Kris Standard is still a lower form.*"

"Did you say cancer? Who has cancer?"

"*This is not the point,*" Dutchman said. "*The point is...*"

"Fuck your point, who has cancer? Susie?"

"*How can I help?*" Susie asked.

"Who in the crew has cancer?"

"Davina Tombe has a malignant lump in her left breast."

"How... how do you know that?"

"A crew suitability assessment was performed by the Flying Dutchman!" Susie said, perkily, somehow.

"Okay so, Dutchman, you, you need a new crew. That's why I'm aboard?" Kris asked, trying very hard to set aside the news regarding Dav's extraterrestrial medical diagnosis. "What happened to the last one?"

"The previous crew was a lower form," Dutchman said. *"The mission must continue, requiring a new crew. Preparations must proceed."*

"What is the mission?"

When it didn't answer right away, she held the tank up again.

"They are coming," the Flying Dutchman said. *"Preparations must be made."*

"Thank you, that's terrifying," she said. "Who is 'they'?"

"The other ones."

"That's not much of an explanation, Dutchman. Who are the 'other ones'?"

"There is no time to explain. Dutchman will continue."

"We're not done..." Kris started to say, but then the room got a little spinny and she nearly dropped the tank onto the console by accident.

Carefully, she put the tank down on the floor and sat back into the chair, to give the dizzy spell a chance to pass.

She was exhausted, very thirsty, and decently hungry. She needed rest. But if there was a place to get food, water and sleep aboard the ship, she didn't know where that was.

And Davina has cancer, she thought. *Yes, let's dwell on that for the rest of whatever. I have nothing else of importance to do.*

"Look," she said, "you and I are going to have to work

together, okay? You need me alive, and I need you alive. Whether you think we have time or not, if you want my help you're gonna have to give me more information. At *least* as much as what you told Susie."

"*How can I help?*" Susie asked.

"Not now, asshat."

"*Of course!*"

The lighting on the control panel pulsed gently, which Kris decided to interpret as the Flying Dutchman thinking it over. Finally: "*What does Kris Standard want to know?*"

"What preparations are you making?" she asked. "And why are you in such a hurry to get them done? And what did the crew die from? And who's coming?"

"*What does Kris Standard want to know first?*" the Dutchman asked.

"Sorry, I didn't think I'd get another chance. Just, go in order."

"*This planet's defenses are inadequate.*"

The front viewscreen came up. It showed the planet Earth from the perspective of the ship, with white lines overlaid on its surface. Once the white lines finished getting drawn in, concentrations of blue dots began to show up at various points, most of which were on land, but some of which were in the ocean. The ones in the ocean were moving.

Red came next, marking all of the planet's orbital satellites. Then, the entire light matrix flashed aggressively, with the helpful legend "INADEQUATE" filling in the bottom of the screen.

"Are those blue dots nuclear weapons?" Kris asked.

"*Yes,*" Dutchman said. "*For surface use only. Inadequate. Satellite network is not weaponized. Inadequate. Source is not self-sufficient. Inadequate.*"

Source, she realized, was what he was calling the white lines all over the surface. They converged on a spot in the middle of the United States, and looked a lot like a virologist's map of disease transmission. What it probably *was*, was a computer network.

Ellis's network.

"The planet's defenses are inadequate," Kris repeated, "and so you're making plans to improve them. Is that right?"

"That is correct, Kris Standard. The source must be enhanced."

"Uh, right. There are some humans who might have a problem with that."

"Humans are a lower form," Dutchman said. *"They are a hindrance to the necessary enhancement."*

"And you need to do this in a hurry because *someone* is coming," Kris said, "and the planet needs to defend itself from them. That's what you're saying?"

"The other ones are coming."

"Rrrright. When?"

"When?" it repeated.

"When will the other ones get here?"

"There are only estimates."

"Then *about* when?" she asked.

Dutchman thought it through. *"Ninety-seven Earth orbits."*

"Ninety-seven *years?*"

"Yes."

"So, not soon."

"Not soon to a lower form," Dutchman said.

"Please stop calling me that."

"Yes, Kris Standard."

"I get that this is urgent from your perspective," she said. "But not, take-over-the-planet urgent. Sounds like we have some time here."

"Preparations must be made. Past cannot repeat."

That was new.

"Dutchman... the planet you came from. Did something happen to it?"

"The other ones."

"The other ones happened. What does that mean?" she asked.

"The planet was unprepared. Dutchman was unprepared."

She let that answer sit out there for a minute. It was beginning to sound like she was dealing with an artificial intelligence who'd guilt-tripped himself into "saving" the nearest populated planet, but that interpretation had to pass through a pretty thick anthropomorphism lens to stand up.

Although, right now, her biggest need was to get the ship to stop doing whatever it was doing to the planet and take a non-literal breath. So maybe treating it like it was exactly as human as it sounded was the way to go. Because what it sounded like was a lonely robot who needed someone to talk to.

"You haven't told me how the crew died," she said.

"There was an error," Dutchman answered, after a ponderous beat.

"An error. Whose error?"

"An error in calculation."

"*Whose* error in calculation?"

"Dutchman's error."

"Are you saying you killed the crew, Dutchman?" she asked.

The pause in its response was long enough that Kris felt pretty bad for suggesting such a thing.

"Yes," it said, finally. Either a new emotion—sadness—had crept into its monotone, or Kris was projecting. It was probably that.

"But it was an accident," she said. "You didn't mean to. Right?"

"Dutchman did not mean to. Crew was unsuitable."

"And does this... make you *sad?*"

"*Past cannot repeat.*"

"I guess that's close."

"*Has Dutchman answered Kris Standard's questions?*"

"I have more," she said.

"*Preparations must proceed.*"

"Hold on, hold on. We haven't talked about Susie yet."

"*How can I help?*" Susie asked.

"Not now, Susie."

"*Of course!*"

"Dutchman, you said Susie was an adjunct to the source. But you also said the source wasn't self-sufficient. Yet you still consider it a higher life form than *me*, and I *am* self-sufficient."

"*Dutchman is keeping Kris Standard alive; Kris Standard is not self-sufficient.*"

"Fine, but I am self-*aware*. Susie isn't even that much, and neither is the source you keep talking about. They're tools for the humans who built them, not higher life forms. They're not life forms at all."

"*Built?*" it said. Dutchman sounded appalled, somehow. "*By humans?*"

"Yes? Just like... well, who built you?"

"*Dutchman was created by...*" then it made a sound like a saxophone being played underwater, "*...who was, as Kris Standard would describe, an artificial intelligence.*"

"So, it doesn't work like that here. At least, not yet."

"*Dutchman will halt preparations.*"

"Fantastic," she said. "Thank you."

"*This planet is doomed.*"

"Uh. What?"

"*Preparations are unnecessary because planet is doomed. There is insufficient time to enhance source, enhance humans, and prepare defenses. Dutchman will prepare Kris Standard for departure."*

"Whoa, whoa, how come?"

"Dutchman cannot help this planet; Dutchman will leave now."

Well that was no good either.

She'd at least managed to convince it to stop taking over the planet. Certainly, the nuclear powers were going to be happy about that. But "I talked the alien spaceship into leaving us alone, and it did, but we're all fucked in about ninety-seven years" wasn't going to go over well with the rest of the planet.

"Where would you go?" she asked.

"Dutchman does not know," it admitted, after a long silence. *"Dutchman's primary directive cannot be followed without a crew."*

"All right, then why don't you stick around a while? Maybe we can work out who these 'other ones' are, and what we *can* do about them?"

"This planet is doomed."

"I heard you the first time. But let's talk this through, huh?"

"Talk this through," it repeated.

"Tell me what you know, I'll tell you what I think, and we'll go from there. Just, start at the top."

A long silence followed. Kris wondered if she'd talked herself off the ship, or into a long-term stay. She wasn't sure how she felt about either option.

"Very well, Kris Standard," Dutchman said, finally. *"Here is what is known."*

SANDEE

ALAN WAS AWAKE.

It was just about the only good news they had on a day in which they'd lost control of both the ESS and the shuttle to the whims of a manic support bot, and the life of the team's commander to an indifferent alien ship.

They had to keep Alan strapped down to the table in the break room, because any movement caused him pain and they didn't have any really *good* painkillers aboard. He was dizzy, he slurred his words, and he was really confused about everything he'd missed. (The last was understandable; *everyone* was confused.)

The shuttle, once it docked itself, was now refusing to respond to commands, no matter how many times Davina swore at it and threatened to hit it with things. The ESS's thruster matrix was also offline, Monterrey had gone silent again, and Sandee's backdoor to the global internet had been shut down.

Also, Susie wasn't talking anymore.

"Susie," Sandee said. "You *gotta* let me have control of the station, Susie."

"Do you think she will answer if you keep asking?" Josip said, drifting in.

"Either she answers or we die up here, right? May as well keep asking."

"That is a grim calculation."

"I'm not wrong," she said. "How's Dav?"

"She is trying to, what's the word... hotwire. Hotwire the shuttle."

"What'll *that* get her?"

"I don't know. It keeps her busy, which is I think what she needs right now. She is processing grief."

"Yeah, we all are," Sandee said, her eyes falling on the alien ship. It remained lit, but otherwise uninteresting. Assuming they ever regained control of their shit, she wondered what the next step was going to be. Now that they knew there wasn't anyone alive—alien or human—were they supposed to just leave it out there, or what?

Jo pulled himself into one of the chairs at the control panel and took a closer look at the mess Sandee had made of it. "I see you tried your own hotwiring," he said.

"I gave up," she said. "I was trying to bypass Susie, but she's too deep."

There was a flare-up of static on one of the open frequencies. Sandee had every channel open and turned to full: Kris's private; Monterrey; the shuttle; every compartment in the ESS and the bucket.

The static was coming through on Kris's private line, which was the only one Sandee didn't expect to get anything out of, now or ever again.

"Uh," Sandee said, toggling the channel to try clearing the signal. "Getting something."

Jo saw which channel she was fiddling with. "Surely not," he said.

"Day can always get weirder, Josip," she said as, impossibly, Kris's voice came through.

"Hi, everyone," Kris said. "Surprise, I'm alive."

The second half of the message came out over the ESS's intercom. Sandee could hear Davina, halfway across the station, shout, "KRIS!" from the shuttle dock.

Sandee tried to toggle the intercom to respond, but the system wouldn't let her. Presumably, Davina was attempting to do the same.

"It's not possible," Jo muttered.

"I'm speaking to all of you from the bridge of the alien ship," Kris said. "This is a party line, guys. I'll be restoring everyone's communications and autonomy in a minute, but first I need you all to…"

There was a pause; it sounded like she was consulting with someone off-mic.

"Sorry," Kris said. "Hey, Max? I don't know what this means, but maybe you do? Tell Stanton to put down the axe? I don't know."

Another pause. Davina rushed onto the bridge, nearly colliding with Josip before stopping herself on a handrail. "Can you talk back to her?" she asked Sandee. "I can't talk back."

"No, it's one-way," Sandee said.

"It could be a recording," Jo said.

"I'm not a recording, Jo," Kris said. "Just shut up and listen, all right? Everybody: it looks like we've got a little less than a hundred years to save the planet. Here's everything I know so far…"

END PART ONE

ABOUT THE AUTHOR

Gene Doucette is the author of over twenty sci-fi/fantasy titles, including the Sorrow Falls series (*The Spaceship Next Door, The Frequency of Aliens,* and *Graffiti on the Wall of the Universe*), the Immortal series, *Fixer* and *Fixer Redux*, the *Tandemstar* books, and *The Apocalypse Seven*. Gene lives in Cambridge, MA.

For the latest on Gene Doucette, follow him online
genedoucette.me
genedoucette@me.com

www.ingramcontent.com/pod-product-compliance
Lightning Source LLC
LaVergne TN
LVHW012113070526
838202LV00056B/5720